THE
LAW
OF
LINES

THE
LAW
OF
LINES

a novel

HYE-YOUNG PYUN

Translated from the Korean by
SORA KIM-RUSSELL

ARCADE PUBLISHING • NEW YORK

First English-language Edition

Originally published in Korean under the title 선의 법칙. (*Seonui beopchik*) by Munhakdongne

This book was translated and published with the support of a generous grant from the Daesan Foundation, Seoul.

Arcade Publishing books may be purchased in bulk at special discounts for sales promotion, corporate gifts, fund-raising, or educational purposes. Special editions can also be created to specifications. For details, contact the Special Sales Department, Arcade Publishing, 307 West 36th Street, 11th Floor, New York, NY 10018 or arcade@skyhorsepublishing.com.

Arcade Publishing® is a registered trademark of Skyhorse Publishing, Inc.®, a Delaware corporation.

Visit our website at www.arcadepub.com.

10 9 8 7 6 5 4 3 2 1

Library of Congress Cataloging-in-Publication Data

Names: P'yŏn, Hye-yŏng, 1972– author. | Kim-Russell, Sora, translator.
Title: The law of lines : a novel / Hye-young Pyun ; translated from the
    Korean by Sora Kim-Russell.
Other titles: Sŏn ŭi pŏpch'ik. English
Description: First edition | New York : Arcade Publishing, [2020]
Identifiers: LCCN 2019055519 (print) | LCCN 2019055520 (ebook) | ISBN
    9781948924962 (hardcover) | ISBN 9781948924979 (ebook)
Classification: LCC PL994.67.H94 S6613 2020 (print) | LCC PL994.67.H94
    (ebook) | DDC 895.73/5—dc23
LC record available at https://lccn.loc.gov/2019055519
LC ebook record available at https://lccn.loc.gov/2019055520

Cover design by Erin Seaward-Hiatt
Cover illustration: © SasinParaksa/Getty Images (skyline); © Happyfoto/Getty Images (texture)

Printed in the United States of America

THE
LAW
OF
LINES

1

Their house was small and run-down. It had been built just two years after Se-oh was born, but already the construction was outdated, the timbers swollen, hinges rusted from years of wind and rain. Fine cracks had appeared on the outsides of the walls and were cemented over. With every summer and winter, the utility bills grew higher as the old house grew worse at keeping out the heat and cold. But despite its flaws, it was still the coziest, warmest world for Se-oh Yun.

Whenever Se-oh's errands took her far from home or kept her out for too long, she broke into a nervous sweat. It was the same now. The long subway ride had left her drenched; when she finally stepped out onto the platform, the air was cool and refreshing. But the effect was momentary. Soon she was shivering. She blamed the new coat. Though the news claimed it was getting warmer, the coat was still too thin for the weather. The end of March wasn't so much the start of spring as it was the last gasp of winter.

Se-oh stopped and took her old, padded coat out of the shopping bag. She'd worn it on the way to the department store. The coat was nice and heavy, but what warmed her more was the thought that she was nearly home.

Traffic was at a standstill, the cars blocked by a crowd of pedestrians in the middle of the street. Their voices were nearly loud enough to drown out the blaring of horns. What had happened? She could feel everyone's eyes on her. Could sense them stopping mid-sentence to stare at her. Stepping back to open a path before she could get too close. Turning their heads when her eyes met theirs. Whispering to the people next to them.

Of course, if she'd actually found the courage to lift her head and look, she would have seen that the others barely registered her presence, but she couldn't manage it. Se-oh let her head drop further and further. Any moment now someone was going to recognize her and grab her by the throat or curse at her and demand to know where she'd been hiding. She hurried away from them.

She didn't get far before she saw the smoke. A thick column of it, which she would have seen immediately if she'd only kept her head up, loomed over the neighborhood. She heard sirens. The fire trucks weren't just pulling up; they'd been sitting in one spot, blaring away, for some time. The ominous wail seemed to fade, as if exhausting the last of its strength, and yet it wasn't moving away from her. She was headed directly for it. When she realized the sirens were in front of her house, she felt her stomach turn.

The crowd was getting louder. Se-oh pushed her way through. The air smelled acrid. Someone ran toward her and shouted for her to be careful. The black smoke struggled to distance itself from the earth.

She walked slowly past the real estate office at the head of the alley. There was usually a yellow dog sitting out front, but she didn't see it this time. The dog belonged to #153. After the owner moved away and abandoned the dog, the neighbors had taken turns feeding it. In return, it kept watch over their alley. She wondered where it had gone. But when she looked back, the dog was right there, as always. It was strange how the dog did not bark at the throngs of people, or wag its tail at Se-oh, or sprawl on the ground and laze about. The dog stood quietly, like a grown-up, among the loudly chattering people.

Se-oh stared at the unbarking dog and shivered with renewed force. It was definitely a bad idea to have worn the new coat on her way home. New clothes should only be worn on a new day. And now, by wearing this coat, she would be forced to ring in a day unlike any she had experienced so far. Why did her father have to go and do something he'd never done before? He'd gone twenty-seven years without buying her clothes for her birthday, so why start now?

The dog was still silent. It stared at Se-oh and did not bark. She took her time, trying to remember whether the dog had always been that quiet, whether it had ever just stared at her like that. She walked a little farther and looked back again: the dog had slumped to the ground in exhaustion.

2

Se-oh was eight when she lost her mother. Her grandmother was the one who had fetched her from school the day it happened.

During the funeral, Se-oh paid very close attention to what everyone did. Watching and filing everything away in her memory was all she could do, as the mother who had always been by her side was gone, her grandmother seemed to have lost the will even to stand up, and her father's spirit had all but left his body.

Se-oh could still recall the grassy scent of the flowers that surrounded her mother's funeral portrait, the smoke from the incense that she could see spiraling up if she stared very hard, the smell of the incense that tingled the tip of her nose, the fiery spice of the beef soup served in the funeral home dining hall, and the taste of the honey-filled rice cakes that popped open as she chewed them.

Her father had always had something to say to Se-oh, but on that day, he said nothing at all and only pinned a white ribbon to her hair. Occasionally, if she started to fret, he gave her a little hug. Even then his lips were sealed. He did not look her in the eye and say something tender. The grown-ups patted Se-oh on the head. To escape their sweaty palms, she twisted away each time she saw a hand come up. Some of the grown-ups even insisted on picking her up in their arms. It used to tickle when they did that, but on that day, it did not. Maybe it was because of the smell of the incense. She couldn't get away from it; the smell made her nose sting and her insides churn. Though she did not cry, she felt as if tears were falling.

Her father sat in his black suit and jumped up to bow whenever more people dressed in black came to pay their respects. When they left, he sat down again, as dumb as a sack. Every now and then he would go over to where people were eating the spicy beef soup and would accept an offer of alcohol. Some of the mourners stayed all night; they broke into groups to play cards. They laughed and ate and chattered loudly. Her father curled up beside them, looking exhausted, and slept.

Then her father took Se-oh to the room where her mother lay. Her mother, dressed in heavy, yellowish clothes, did not stir. The stiff, uncomfortable-looking fabric of her mother's burial clothes and the hard, angry look on her mother's face frightened Se-oh and made her burst into tears. Still, her mother did not move. Relatives encircled her mother. Her father gave Se-oh another brief hug before placing her hand in her cousin's hand and sending them both out of the room.

She heard the heavy door shut behind them. It wasn't until much later that she learned what else had happened behind that closed door to the body of the deceased dressed in those thick hemp clothes.

Her cousin did not take Se-oh far. The girl was older by only three or four years, so she might have been too afraid to leave the long, empty hallway. They sat side by side and listened to Se-oh's father and their relatives cry in the room they'd just left. Her cousin sniffled and covered Se-oh's ears with her hands. The hallway grew silent, like the air when it snows. The silence mingled with the sound of stifled tears. She'd thought at first that the sound was coming from the people in the room, but it was coming from her cousin.

"What happened to Mom?" She waited a long time to ask that question aloud. Her father kept rinsing the soapy dishes and pretended not to hear her. "What happened to Mom?" She asked the question again, and only then did he turn off the tap, remove the rubber gloves, kneel down, and gently grasp Se-oh's small shoulders. He regarded her quietly and stroked her hair.

He did not start to say, "Your mom . . ." His throat was not choked with sobs. He did not tell her, with a sad look in his eyes, "She isn't coming home anymore." He did not say, "She's asleep underground." He merely looked at her and hugged her tightly.

Because of that gentle silence, she never asked again. He held her lightly by the shoulders for a moment before letting go and standing back up. He turned his back to her, put the rubber gloves back on, turned on the water as high as it would go, and noisily finished washing the dishes.

These experiences made Se-oh think she knew what death was. Death was wearing uncomfortable clothes and lying on a hard bed. Death was listening to the tears of those close to you. Talking about death meant meeting each other's eyes in stony silence or disguising the sound of your tears with a loudly running tap.

Someone brushed past Se-oh as she stood there staring blankly. She snapped back into the moment. In front of her, paramedics carried a person on a stretcher, and she wondered if that person was her father. If the person on the stretcher *was* her father, then she wanted to see what he was wearing. *Please don't let it be something heavy and uncomfortable*, she thought.

Before the stretcher drew near, someone grabbed Se-oh's shoulder.

"Are you okay?"

The question was how Se-oh knew everything was not okay. The face looked familiar. It seemed to belong to one of her neighbors, but she could not remember whose. It could have been a stranger. A police officer. Maybe a paramedic. The person grabbed Se-oh's right arm. They wanted to stop her from going into the house. There was no need. Se-oh was standing still.

Before the ambulance door closed, the blanket fluttered, and she caught a glimpse of the person on the stretcher. It wasn't him. The thought brought her no relief.

3

Ki-jeong Shin was in the middle of grading homework when she was summoned by the principal. Until becoming a teacher, she'd never realized that it meant only occasional teaching and frequent busywork. When she added up all the busywork she had to complete before the end of the week, there were over a dozen separate things she had to deal with. The first was grading. Not because it was the most important but because it was in her way.

She had assigned the students to work in groups to write travel guides and give presentations, and now her desk was buried under piles of paper. She was already sick of grading. She didn't have to look to know that they'd copied everything from Wikipedia and printed photos off of other people's blogs. The only show of effort that any of them had bothered to put into the assignment was printing the photos in color.

She was on the third packet when the call came from the principal. The unexpected had a way of intruding on ordinary things sometimes. Like this unwanted summons.

The head teacher from Class 3 was in the principal's office. After a moment, the vice principal came in looking stern, with

9

Do-jun Weon and another student in tow. When Do-jun saw Ki-jeong looking quizzically at him, he lowered his face.

A grocery store near the school had been shoplifted. Nine conspirators in total. Over the past few months, a group of students who attended the same after-school prep classes had been going in groups of two, four, and six into the store, where the owner worked alone, and systematically shoplifting items. Suspicious as to why the till was never adding up, the owner had installed a closed-circuit camera and discovered that it was the doing of students from the nearby cram school. The police said they'd caught students stealing from stationery stores and other shops in front of the school plenty of times before, but this was the first time it had been carried out so systematically and with so many accomplices.

Ki-jeong was shocked to hear Do-jun was among them. Do-jun's family was well-off. His parents ran their own business. She had her suspicions that it might be something unsavory, as they never went into detail about what line of business they were in. Last year, the head teacher had told her that Do-jun's parents had made a sizable contribution to the school. Unless his parents were unusually strict about not giving him an allowance, he should have had no reason to resort to stealing.

Ki-jeong gazed with interest at Do-jun's lowered head. She did not think highly of him, perhaps because she had witnessed the boy acting in self-serving ways before. He was unreliable, always chasing after girls and goofing off when everyone was supposed to be working together to clean the classroom. And yet, he cared enough about his grades that if he forgot to bring his homework, he would go hungry in order to run home at lunchtime and get it. For their group assignment, he'd let his teammates do all the work but took all the credit for it in his presentation, much to their resentment. He might have gotten away with it if she hadn't over-heard them whispering about it. As far as Ki-jeong could tell, Do-jun never did anything that might bring him harm, took the credit when it served him, and ignored anything that didn't.

The fact that he was so comfortable with her was also strangely aggravating. Do-jun stopped by her classroom every day to give her something. Mostly it was snacks, but other times he'd give her toothpaste or soap or some other small item. Before Ki-jeong could even react, he would say, "Come on, don't be shy! Just take it." While she was at a loss for words at how forward he was, he would say, "Shall I bring you something else instead?" which made her angry. She had a feeling it wouldn't be long before he was handing her an envelope of cash, and because of this thing that had not even happened, she kept the boy at arm's length.

Do-jun seemed to catch on. He'd gradually begun to play the part of a well-behaved and trustworthy student. He cleaned the windows in the hallway and helped other students to move desks aside to mop the floor. But even then, she did not doubt for one minute that he only did these things when she was around to witness them.

She thought she should pull Do-jun aside some time and give him a stern talking to, but she kept putting it off. He hadn't exactly done anything wrong. Since the things he brought her were not expensive and could either be eaten or used and tossed, it seemed that if she scolded him, she would only make it obvious that she simply didn't like him.

She shared the snacks he gave her with her fellow teachers. She didn't mind all that much when they teased her for being popular. As for the toothpaste and hand cream and other items, she tucked those away in a paper bag. Whenever she ran out of something, she replaced it with an item that Do-jun had given her without a second thought. When he'd brought her slippers a short while back, Ki-jeong had realized how observant he was. Just the day before, one of the slippers she wore indoors at work had ripped. The pair he'd given her weren't expensive. They had an obviously fake logo of a foreign brand printed on the instep.

She had thanked him, for the first time. He'd grinned bashfully. When she saw how innocent he seemed, she'd felt a little sorry for having thought so badly of the things he did, when he was obviously doing them just to get attention.

Ki-jeong brought Do-jun from the principal's office to the teachers' lounge and sat him down across from her with a sigh. The boy hung his head low, as if her sigh were weighing down the air in the room. The pale nape of his neck was exposed, revealing a round, thumbnail-sized birthmark near the top of his spine. Ki-jeong stared hard at the birthmark. It was big enough to catch her eye, and yet she had never noticed it before. The boy had fair skin without any of the usual pimples, and he must have had braces at a young age because his teeth were very straight.

It occurred to her then why she disliked him so much. The boy had the confidence and arrogance unique to those born lucky. The kind of luck that meant having rich parents and a nice house and being able to buy new things anytime you wanted and never having to worry about how you were going to make a future for yourself.

"Look at me."

Do-jun hesitated before lifting his head. The blood had rushed to his face, making him a little flushed.

"Why'd you do it?"

She asked the question gently, but the boy didn't answer. She had expected as much, so she wasn't disappointed. No child would feel inclined to immediately blurt out that they were led astray by bad kids and then name the ringleader. Fifteen was the age at which you started to learn that blaming everything on someone else was both the easiest and the hardest thing to do. Ki-jeong had to avoid injuring the boy's sense of pride while helping him explain to her why he'd gone along with the ringleader. The teachers at the other schools would likewise be coaxing their students in whatever way they needed in order to avoid having the ringleader turn out to be from their school. The truth of what had happened would turn on whoever told the most convincing story first.

Ki-jeong decided to stall. She would tire the boy out with a long silence and then soften him up by saying things like, I'm just disappointed that you let me down, and, This isn't who you are, and, You've made things really difficult for me. If that didn't work, she would try scaring him instead. She would talk about the police, or pressing charges, or she would mention juvie. Then Do-jun would make some exaggerated and obvious excuses about how it was all the fault of the other kids.

"Look at him sitting there, saying nothing," said a fellow teacher who taught trigonometry and had a desk next to hers in the teachers' lounge. "As if he did something to be proud of! How much did the little son of a bitch steal?"

Trig gave the boy a hard smack on the head. Do-jun's head sank further. Ki-jeong let out a sigh just as Trig plunked back down in his chair.

"Do you want my help, Ms. Shin? Words don't work on brats like these. You gotta rough 'em up."

Ki-jeong didn't answer.

"You'll never catch a thief by acting soft, you're not his pediatrician. With brats like that, you gotta think like you're in homicide. Act like a cop."

Trig was so loud that other teachers nearby burst into laughter, and they all started cracking jokes: "Homicide sounds like a good career move for Ms. Shin!" "You didn't know? She moonlights as a detective!" Ki-jeong chose to ignore them.

Trig loved sticking his nose into everything. He was always rapping the heads of students who'd been called before other teachers and lecturing them. He thought of it as playing bad cop, but he didn't realize how much it weakened the other teachers' authority. Ki-jeong tried to hide the fact that she couldn't stand him by keeping her words kind and friendly, but this only invited more interference from him.

"Ms. Shin, you want me to introduce you to a good friend in homicide? He's tall and good-looking. Got a bit of a temper. But he behaves himself when he's around a pretty girl. I wonder if he'd behave himself with you."

Trig chuckled. Ki-jeong turned her head so he couldn't see her openly sneering at him. When she looked back at Do-jun, her conscience pricked at her. The boy was staring right at her. He looked relaxed. She wasn't sure if he was thinking that he'd paid fairly for his crime by taking a rap on the head from Trig, or if Trig's teasing of Ki-jeong had given him courage, or if he'd seen Ki-jeong sneering at Trig.

"Well? Why'd you do it?" she asked in a low but tense voice.

"The bitch is nuts."

Do-jun looked right at her as he said it. Ki-jeong was shocked; she thought at first that the boy was talking about her.

"What? How dare you speak that way to a grown-up!" Trig

bellowed from behind Ki-jeong. Ki-Jeong frowned. She regretted not having used the counseling office instead. Both the counseling office and teachers' lounge were designated for one-on-one talks with students and were intended to avoid the kind of unsavory incident that could arise when a teacher and student were alone together without closed-circuit cameras.

"Who's nuts?"

"The old lady who owns the grocery store."

"Why is she nuts?"

"Because she went nuts and called me a thief."

"She called you a thief because you stole from her," Ki-jeong said coolly.

"For fuck's sake!" Do-jun looked Ki-jeong dead in the eye. "I swear I didn't steal anything that time! I was handing her my money when Hyeong-cheol ran outside saying he had to answer his cell phone, and then all of a sudden the lady starts screaming, 'Thief!' That's when she ran after Hyeong-cheol. Then she started calling me a thief, too. I was just standing there."

"Who's Hyeong-cheol?"

"A friend of mine. We go to the same cram school. His grades are damn good."

The curse words Do-jun usually suppressed in order to seem well-behaved kept slipping out. He even added details that she hadn't asked for. She could tell he was starting to get worked up. Ki-jeong relaxed.

"Was he in on it?"

"We didn't steal anything."

"Not that time, you mean."

"Right."

"So?"

15

"That's what happened."

"*So?*"

"What?"

The boy stalled as he tried to figure out what he was supposed to say. Ki-jeong quickly asked, "Did you steal?"

"No, I—"

"You're innocent, right?"

"I didn't steal nothing, but I got called a thief and hit over the head and yelled at. Hyeong-cheol, goddammit, that lady broke his glasses. She hit him in the face. Everyone walking by saw it. So fucking embarrassing . . . That bitch is always like that. Freaks out and calls everyone a thief. Then she grabs you without even bothering to check if you're the one who stole, and just starts hitting you and cussing you out."

"Oh, what a performance! Bravo!" Trig interrupted again. "Listen, you little shit, you think it's okay to steal just because you feel wronged?"

He rapped Do-jun on the head with his knuckles, and the boy swore under his breath. Trig ignored it and walked away. Ki-jeong said nothing. She found herself wishing Do-jun were a little worse at controlling his anger. What a shame. She wouldn't have minded seeing him take a swing at Trig.

"How'd the group form?"

"She's been mean to a lot of kids."

"So you banded together? To get revenge?"

"That wasn't it . . ."

"Whose idea was it? Yours?"

"No, I swear! I joined them later. Cross my heart."

Now that the story was out, the boy seemed at a loss as to what he should say. It wasn't as if it were some terrible sin to swipe a pack of gum or a bag of chips because you resented being falsely accused of stealing. The problem was that he had shoplifted over and over, in a team, over a long period of time, and the school couldn't just let that go.

"Why did you keep stealing?"

Having cornered the boy, Ki-jeong finally got around to the key question. She left off the part where she wanted to say, You're supposed to stop *before* you get caught. Teachers weren't supposed to say things like that.

"Because I didn't get caught," Do-jun said nonchalantly.

In other words, the only reason it went so far was because he hadn't been stopped sooner.

"What on earth did you steal?"

This time, she kept her voice low. She didn't want anyone to hear the question. It seemed to her that asking for all these details was the job of the police, not a teacher.

"Just small stuff."

"Too much to remember?"

"Nothing special."

"What was the first thing you stole?"

The boy let out a sigh and answered, "Batteries."

"And the second thing?"

"I don't remember."

"Then try to list as much as you can."

"It really was small stuff."

"What'd you do with the stuff you stole?"

"I gave it to poor kids."

"Poor kids?"

"You know, those kids who look like they got nothing. I gave it to them. I didn't keep it for myself."

Do-jun put on an expression that seemed to say he was a true philanthropist.

"'Kids who look like they got nothing'?"

He grinned bashfully. He was confident he'd done nothing wrong. Ki-jeong spoke firmly as she prepared to confront the boy with his crimes.

"You've bred quite the accomplices."

"Accomplices?"

"Yes, accomplices. Those who committed the crime with you. Your friends who didn't steal are now accomplices because of you. The things you shoplifted, that's all stolen property. And accepting stolen property, even if you didn't steal it yourself, makes you an accomplice."

"Really? Great! That's what I thought." Do-jun chuckled. "Because *now* I remember what I stole."

"Tell me."

"Those."

Do-jun pointed at Ki-jeong's slippers. The expression on his face was the exact opposite of when he had pleaded that he'd only stolen out of resentment at being falsely accused.

"And there's more. Perioe toothpaste. Chupa Chups lollipops. Boddo crackers. Choco Songi cookies. Baked potato chips. Highlighter pens. Garglin mouthwash. Febreze. Rice soap. Or was it barley soap? Whatever. Soap."

Do-jun looked her dead in the eye as he spoke. Now that he was on a roll, he was recalling everything he'd ever given to Ki-jeong along with the slippers. Perhaps he'd been too caught off guard to remember, but now that she'd mentioned accomplices and stolen property, it was coming right back to him.

Or maybe not.

As much as she wanted to believe otherwise, he had to have planned it this way. He'd known from the start that it would blow up like this, and that was why he'd kept giving her little things every day. He wasn't seeking attention or making up for a lack of affection; his goal from the very start was to turn a teacher into an accomplice. Out of boredom. What a sly and vicious child.

The fake brand logo on the instep of her slippers grated at her. She had thanked Do-jun for them, unaware that they were stolen. She had worn stolen goods while walking all over the school and meeting with students' parents. She had worn stolen goods while reading Baek Seok's poetry in class and taught the structure of expository writing with an essay on ocean ecosystems. She had worn stolen goods while instructing her students to write an essay on ethics and responsibility, and had graded the results.

She wanted to rip the slippers off of her feet and whack the boy over the head with them, but she couldn't. She was interrupted by her cell phone ringing from its perch atop a pile of homework to be graded. Ki-jeong was relieved by the timely phone call. Thanks to whoever was calling, no one would catch her losing her temper. No one would know how upset she was by what the boy had told her.

Do-jun raised his head stiffly but then leaned back in the chair and made himself comfortable. As the cell phone kept ringing, he even made a show of crossing his arms. Ki-jeong slowly answered it. Her plan was to buy herself a little time in this war of nerves. If she was too short with the person on the other end, Do-jun would see at once that he was getting to her.

"Hello, I'm looking for a Ki-jeong Shin."

It was obvious who was calling. A delivery person or the like. Most people who called addressed her as Ms. Shin or Teacher Shin. Faculty colleagues or students' parents.

"Who is this?"

Ki-jeong kept her voice deliberately cold. The boy still had his arms crossed and was leisurely looking around the office. The moment she got off the phone, she didn't care who saw or not, or whether she would get a lecture from the principal later about how corporal punishment was strictly forbidden no matter the circumstances or not, she was going to take that slipper off and beat him silly over the head with it.

"This is the police."

"The police?"

Ki-jeong glanced at Do-jun. The boy flinched. She watched as he slowly released his arms. Ki-jeong kept her eyes on him as she asked, "What seems to be the matter, Officer?"

What came out of the officer's mouth next was, to her surprise, the name of her younger sister. The moment she heard that name, she had a premonition that her becoming an accomplice to some pipsqueak thief and having worn stolen property would soon seem like nothing at all.

After listening to the officer, she brought one hand up to cover her face. Do-jun looked terrified.

Ki-jeong quietly ended the call. The hand that held the phone was trembling. She was barely able to muster the strength to address the boy seated in front of her.

"Leave."

"Leave?"

He sounded incredulous. Ki-jeong nodded weakly. The boy muttered something. She didn't respond. A loud noise was beginning to wail inside her ears. The sound was coming from her own living body. Ki-jeong focused on that unpleasant sound to the exclusion of all else.

The boy raised his finger and drew circles by the side of his head before jumping up from the chair and rushing out of the room. Ki-jeong pretended not to hear any of the things he said. She ignored the gesture he made. She would have reacted no differently no matter what he said or did. After hearing what the officer had to tell her, nothing else mattered. According to the officer, a dead body presumed to be her sister's had been found.

4

It is a matter of course that when death overtakes life, the body undergoes a transformation. Ki-jeong had learned this from her father's funeral. Her father had lain on a hard bed, his body yellow and swollen head to toe from the fluid that had built up in his abdominal cavity. His body demonstrating the fact that concluding a life was never easy. The swelling was, in a manner of speaking, death's war trophy in its victory over life.

Her father had been hospitalized for symptoms of jaundice. The jaundice turned out to be caused by cirrhosis of the liver. The cirrhosis worsened rapidly, the fluid in his abdomen refusing to budge no matter how many diuretics were administered. Ki-jeong was twenty-two at the time, her younger sister only nine.

Now the deceased body presumed to belong to her younger sister looked almost nothing like her sister had in life. But Ki-jeong was convinced it was her. She was certain that, just as with her father, death had left its trophy behind. And, as if to tell her that the battle had been more vicious than ever, the condition of her younger sister's body was beyond gruesome.

The corpse had been found in the lower reaches of the Nam

River in the provincial town of J—. A housewife had drowned herself in that river right after a Buddhist lantern festival, and during the search for her, Ki-jeong's sister's body had been recovered instead. It would take some time before her body could be buried. There was still the autopsy, among other necessary procedures. Since no suicide note had been found, the coroners could not confirm the cause of death. That is to say, while it was obvious she had died by drowning, they did not know whether it was a suicide or an accident. Even with an autopsy, they said, they could estimate the approximate time of death, but they might never know the circumstances that had led up to it. While listening patiently to their long-winded explanation, Ki-jeong had already reached the conclusion that her sister had committed suicide. It was bound to happen eventually, she thought; it'd only been a matter of time.

The officer who had escorted Ki-jeong into the morgue was called away to check some documents. He stepped out, leaving just the two of them, Ki-jeong and her sister, alone in that chilly room. Or to put it more accurately, Ki-jeong was alone, the sole life among a roomful of deaths.

When she was face to face with her sister, the thought occurred to her that she had wished for this to happen. For the sister who had tormented her mother her whole life to disappear for good. She tried to deny the thought but couldn't. Nevertheless, she hadn't imagined it would happen quite like this.

No, that wasn't true either.

The truth was she'd imagined it often. Her little sister mangled, charred to black, torn to shreds. That was what made it all the more painful to see the body cold and stiff and so badly damaged.

Her time alone in the morgue with her sister seemed to stretch on forever. The unreal cold chilled her to the bone, reminding her that she and her sister were both made of flesh. And that her sister was now a cold and distant being, a phantom.

Ki-jeong asked her sister as she lay there silently: *What happened?* Her sister didn't stir. Yet she felt as if she heard an answer.

One thing led to another.

If she could have spoken, that's what her sister might have said.

Her sister had been accepted to a university out in Wonju and had moved into the dorms. Ki-jeong thought she could have made it into a better school in or near Seoul, but her sister was stubborn. Ki-jeong didn't do much to dissuade her. At first, her sister had come back to Seoul during school vacations, but eventually she stopped showing up even then. She kept changing her phone number, making it difficult to stay in touch with her. Once, she returned home out of the blue after a year or so of no contact. Ki-jeong and her mother had been inwardly convinced that she'd left for good, so when she came back, they felt both disappointed and relieved.

When she tried to ask her sister where she'd been and what she'd been doing all that time, her sister gave the same non-answer:

One thing led to another.

Ki-jeong knew that, of all laws, this—the way one thing leads invariably to the next—was the only of life's laws she couldn't find fault with. But it was still an upsetting answer. Her sister seemed to leave everything up to luck and chance. It wasn't that one thing led to another, it was that her sister left life to its own devices.

In Ki-jeong's view of things, life was a weed. If you didn't tend to it, it would grow out of control and spread and shove its branches into everything. If you did tend to it, it would be restrained and trimmed and plucked, and, if you did really well, it could even have a shape to it. How could her sister not know that? Especially having been so miserable her whole life. It suddenly occurred to Ki-jeong that the phrase *her whole life* now referred to the past perfect tense where her sister was concerned, and she went blank for a moment.

Her sister had come into Ki-jeong's home, holding Ki-jeong's father's hand, at the age of five, and from that point on, she'd become a burden to Ki-jeong's mother. Ki-jeong's mother was pitiable and terrifying. Her sister was pathetic and shrewd. Her father was irresponsible and cowardly. Ki-jeong consciously tried to treat her sister fairly. She mistakenly believed that she acted as an objective and neutral mediator between her mother and sister. In truth, she was entirely indifferent. *You're not like her,* her mother always said. And because she was not like her, Ki-jeong regarded her sister with pity and sympathized with her with all of her heart.

When her sister returned home after that year of no contact, she'd seemed changed. She was warm to their mother, and when they sat down to dinner, she'd talked nonstop. Ki-jeong and her mother were unable to get a word in. Her mother ended up losing patience and leaving the table. Her sister seemed entirely unconcerned and continued to prattle on, much to Ki-jeong's wonder.

Her sister had always been just as uncomfortable around Ki-jeong as she was around her mother, but upon her return, she acted differently. She pestered Ki-jeong to take her out to popular restaurants, asked Ki-jeong to loan her a bag, wore Ki-jeong's clothes without permission, waited in front of the school when Ki-jeong was scheduled to get off of work, claiming that she'd just happened to be in the neighborhood, and then hit her up for spending money. In a word, she acted like a true little sister.

When vacation ended, her sister returned to school, where she kept herself busy. Or at least according to the occasional updates she gave them over the phone. She belonged to several clubs on campus and never missed a single class. She studied for exams late into the night at the library and went on blind dates. One minute she was joining a mountaineering group and going on a week-long hiking trip, and the next she was joining an a cappella group and horrifying everyone by crooning vocal warm-ups right in the middle of a phone call. During a school break, she announced that she was taking a trip and dropped out of contact for over a month. On another break, she joined an advertising club and came home with a crate-load of a brand of bottled water that had a low market share. She said she was preparing for a copywriting contest and swigged the water constantly before coming up with the ad copy: "We don't bury pigs. We don't bury chickens. We only bury purified water." Ki-jeong couldn't help but grimace when she read it. Her sister added the unasked-for explanation: "It means the water is safe from hoof-and-mouth disease and bird flu. Remember? When all those diseased farm animals were buried and it polluted the groundwater?" When Ki-jeong retorted that that ad alone would make customers sick, her sister changed it to "We don't sell water, we sell class," which made no sense for the brand, which was named after a small hick town out in rural Gangwon Province. Sometimes Ki-jeong thought her sister should act more like a student and loaf around and take it easy, but instead her sister acted like she was making up for lost time, keeping herself busy and distracted with things that, in Ki-jeong's eyes, were not really worth her time.

Now it fell to Ki-jeong to contact people who might have known her sister. So as not to be the only one at her funeral. So as not to abandon her little sister. The very first place she called was her sister's department at the university. They told her that her sister had never re-enrolled. Thinking there must be some mistake, she tried calling the office of the registrar and the student affairs office. They told her the same thing. She wouldn't put it past her sister. Her sister had not been all that interested in her declared major.

After a couple of days, Ki-jeong went in person to her sister's university in Wonju. Her sister could still have attended student club meetings while on a leave of absence. Ki-jeong went first to the mountaineering club's room. There were several photos taped to a metal filing cabinet. Her sister's face was in none of them. Next she went to the advertising club. None of the students there knew her sister's name, but they did confirm that they'd created an ad for bottled water. Ki-jeong remembered the ad copy her sister had written. *We don't sell water, we sell class.* One of the students told her it was the slogan for a famous foreign water company. They added that it had won a great deal of prize money in an ad contest.

She thought the police would be actively investigating her sister's case, but when she called to follow up, they said they were busy. That her case was not pressing. They would decide the course of the investigation after they got the autopsy results. Ki-jeong accepted the fact that her sister's death was just one of many countless deaths to the police. And besides, the sooner they moved forward on it, the sooner her mother would find out. Her mother would have to find out at some point, but now wasn't the time. When she imagined her mother's reaction, Ki-jeong feared what might happen.

At least the police were quick to hand over the call history for the cell phone registered in her sister's name, which Ki-jeong had requested. She wanted to call everyone her sister had been in contact with and invite them to the funeral. Since her sister would be taking her last journey without being seen off by their mother, Ki-jeong wanted it to at least be a little less lonely.

While scanning the list, which wasn't very long, the first number that jumped out at her was her own. All of the calls had been made by her sister. The calls were short, some no more than a second. Her sister had wanted to tell her something, and Ki-jeong hadn't listened. Another number caught her eye. It was the last call made from her sister's phone. Her sister had tried the number over and over. Ki-jeong wanted to tell that person what had happened to her sister. The person whom her sister had dialed repeatedly during her final moments but who, like Ki-jeong, had not answered.

According to the log, those calls were also short—just one, two, three seconds, eleven seconds at the longest. Ki-jeong could think of only one scenario in which you would end a call after one second, and that was hanging up the moment you realize who's calling.

She tried the number using a public phone in the school cafeteria. It made her uncomfortable to reveal her own number to someone she didn't know. She called the number several times, but no one answered.

Where was this number? Who was using it? Who was the person her sister had tried so anxiously to reach? Was it the person who'd led her sister to J— in the first place, where she had no friends or family? Who was this person who answered their phone only to slam the door on her sister's earnest heart after just one or two seconds, eleven seconds at the most?

5

It didn't matter if you were dealing with a victim or a perpetrator, the hardest type of person to deal with was someone like Se-oh Yun. Mutes were worse than liars. No human being can lie all the time, it's not in their nature. The truth is bound to pop out, even right in the middle of telling a lie. Liars made you proud to be able to see through them, but mutes—they only made you boil over with anger.

Se-oh Yun wasn't saying a word. When Detective Myeong-guk Kim asked, "We understand that your father, Su-chang Yun, has been depressed lately?" Se-oh stared at him and smirked. She wasn't answering his question. She was mocking it.

Detective Kim took a photograph from a drawer and handed it to Se-oh. When it came to showing someone evidence and getting them to believe him, he was a pro.

"Look at this."

It was a photograph of the cross section of a gas hose. Se-oh knew at once what it was.

"Pretty clean, huh? This here shows it was cut. Sliced clean with scissors or a knife, on purpose."

The results of the investigation weren't out yet, but Detective

Kim wanted to get a reaction from Se-oh. He wanted to make her start talking. Se-oh stared at the photo. Little changed in her expression. He couldn't stand the silent treatment, but he wasn't going to lose his temper over it either. At least dealing with someone like her was more efficient than people who asked too many pointless questions and had to be told the same thing over and over.

At #157, the gas line, which was anchored to the wall next to the kitchen stove, had broken above the manual valve while the valve was turned off. Normally when the rubber tubing deteriorated, it broke somewhere beneath the valve. Gravity and the passage of time are always hardest to bear at the bottom. This meant that as long as the valve was closed, there would be no gas leak, even if the bottom hose fell off completely. To put it another way, if the bottom hose was broken while the valve was turned on, then there was a good chance the hose was intentionally severed.

Likewise, if the top hose was broken while the valve was off—as was the case at #157—then the odds were high that it was not an accident. It was possible to maliciously fake a worn-out gas hose in order to cause something bad to happen. That had been the case with the recent gas explosion in Uijeongbu not long ago. The gas valve had been turned off and a sharp object used to sever the top hose.

But a similar case alone was not enough to conclude that the explosion in #157 was due to foul play. The cabinet above the sink had been found completely torn from the wall. Accidents had been caused before by kitchen cabinets falling and damaging the gas line. A detailed investigation was needed to determine whether the explosion caused the cabinet to fall, or whether the explosion was caused by the cabinet falling and dislodging the worn-out hose. That would take time. If deteriorated hose, accident; if severed hose, incident.

Se-oh could not believe that the gas line in the photo was the same one installed in their kitchen. She must have seen it several times a day for over twenty years, and yet the shape and color were unfamiliar. Hearing Detective Kim speak so conclusively, so full of assurance, about a gas line she'd never paid attention to before, she was struck by a pessimistic thought: The police would conclude the case as they saw fit. They would not help her father at all.

Though she knew people only said it to comfort her, it enraged Se-oh each time someone said the accident was a stroke of bad luck. That was the kind of thing you said in response to getting an answer wrong on a test or slipping and hurting your tailbone because you weren't paying attention to where you were going.

If this had happened solely due to bad luck, then whose luck was bad? Her father's, who was burned from head to toe in the explosion? Se-oh's, who had missed the explosion and survived, but lost her home and would likely lose her father, too?

Detective Kim didn't believe it was the fault of bad luck. Some accidents were fabricated from a disguise of coincidence and luck, and he regarded this as one of those cases. Se-oh didn't fully understand what he meant by that, but it made her feel worse than hearing it was bad luck.

Detective Kim stared at Se-oh. He seemed to think she hadn't understood him well enough, because he came right up to the desk and sat down.

"There's a thing called a hose cock. Allow me to explain. They're not in use anymore. You can't use them. Gas lines were redesigned to not allow them, because they're dangerous. See, it's real easy to slice right through. The hose is rubber, so it used to happen all the time. But there are a lot of old houses where the gas lines haven't been updated. It's impossible to go door-to-door tracking them all down. Your house, Ms. Yun, was one of those old houses. Makes it real easy to get a gas leak. Once the leak starts, the gas just keeps coming out. That's because it doesn't have one of these. An automatic shut-off valve. The new gas lines all have fuses that shut off right away if it senses there's a leak. Makes it a lot harder for accidents to happen. You get what I'm saying?"

Se-oh nodded. She knew what he was literally saying, but she didn't know what he was driving at. She only nodded because she figured he would keep staring at her until she did.

"There was a similar case not long ago. It was all over the news—did you see it? Up in Uijeongbu. Same as your case."

She remembered. A lot of people had been injured, so there'd been news updates every day. Or maybe there was just nothing else worth reporting on at the time. She'd probably even watched the news with her father. Of course, she couldn't remember what sort of face her father had made or what he'd said.

"These gas explosions—there were over a hundred and fifty last year. Only reason the Uijeongbu case made the news was because so many people died from it. We've already had three cases in our jurisdiction alone. Fact is, the farther out from the city you go, the more of these explosions you get. If you want to lower the suicide rate, all you have to do is add an automatic shut-off valve to the gas line in every last kitchen in the country."

As she looked at Detective Kim, she was reminded suddenly of heading off to work many years earlier. Before leaving the dorm, she and the other team members had all stood in a circle and shouted their motto: "Don't sell, teach!" The image had nothing to do with where she was now, but it struck her that Detective Kim was no different from the people she'd worked with back then. He had it all down to a science. That is, he knew how to get people pumped up, and how to convince them of anything, so he could get exactly what he wanted from them.

"Have you seen this before?"

Detective Kim tapped a photo of a half-burned disposable lighter.

"You find them everywhere, these lighters. Every house has got one or two. It's the sort of thing you think you haven't seen even though you have, or you think you have seen even though you haven't. They're so common that they're useless as evidence. They should make 'em different from each other. Why do they have to make them so damn identical, am I right? Makes our job harder. Your father smokes, doesn't he? Looks like maybe he snipped that hose there and had himself a smoke. We found the lighter in the living room. Along with the cigarette. How's your father been lately? I hear he's been grumbling a lot about dying. . . ."

Se-oh closed her eyes. The world slowly turned into a solid wall. It wasn't dark and dismal. Being surrounded by a wall meant she was safe. What she now understood was that, all this time, while her father had been lying in the hospital, while he was in agony from having his flesh stripped and his bones seared, while his organs were damaged and tubes inserted into him kept him breathing, the police had been doing absolutely nothing. She felt like running away.

"Ms. Yun, I'm going to tell you all about the father you don't know. Listen up. First of all, your father is in debt."

Detective Kim shuffled some papers. Se-oh knew about it

already. She didn't know the details of where all the debt had come from, but she had a pretty good idea.

"Big banks, small banks, usurers—the debtors' holy trinity! That's how it goes. When you can't pay back the big banks, you borrow from the small banks, and when you can't pay back the small banks, you go to the usurers. Do you know what usurers are? Loan sharks. If there were a step after that, he'd have taken it, but sadly for him there's no such thing. The only place left to go after borrowing from loan sharks is up there."

Detective Kim raised his index finger and gestured upward.

"Since he couldn't pay back his loans and kept on lying to everyone and not taking responsibility for his decisions, he probably got mad and argued with his creditors. And then of course he would've turned to crime. According to the people he was friends with back when he owned a tool shop, your father Mr. Su-chang Yun used to say all the time, 'I want to die. The work is killing me. What's the point of living this way?' Not long before the explosion, he asked if anyone knew where he could buy a strong pesticide. You know, the rate of success for suicide among the elderly, it's very, very high. Old folks don't mess around when it comes to deciding whether or not to kill themselves. As soon as they decide they want to go, they really go."

"He wouldn't do that."

Having said that, she felt extremely lonely. But she comforted herself with the thought that she was okay. After all, she wasn't as lonely as her father, who was lying alone in a hospital room wrapped in bandages. She could bear it. No matter how lonely she felt, she was not as lonely as her father.

"Of course not! Of course he wouldn't do that. He wouldn't do that at all." Detective Kim laughed. "But here's the thing. This kind of thing is done all the time by people who would never, ever do such a thing. It's not in our nature as human beings. If humanity consisted solely of people who *would* do that sort of thing, we'd all be terrified to death. But that's the thing about people. It goes against our nature to rape, and yet we do. We would never lie or cheat, but we do. And, of course, no one would ever take their own life, and yet they do."

Detective Kim looked at Se-oh's silent face and stopped talking. In order for him to close the case as a suicide, above all else, the motive had to be clear. In Su-chang Yun's case, it didn't much matter whether you pointed the finger at his depression or his hardships. If the fire were ruled an accident, then he'd have some money coming to him through insurance, albeit not very much. What mattered more was getting the family to agree.

Se-oh gazed at Detective Kim. She vowed to never die alone. If you were alone, you had no walls to hide behind. Her father must have been so lonely lying in that hospital.

"There is someone who arranged to meet with your father that day. Do you know him? Someone who might have come by now and then to collect money. Name is Su-ho Lee. You say you were home all the time? Remember seeing him?"

She had known that someone had been coming to the house looking for money. But she'd never let on to her father that she knew. Her father had wanted to keep it from Se-oh, and so the debt collector had remained a stranger to her. She'd never seen his face. Nor did she know his voice all that well. Her father had always dealt with him out in the courtyard. Very occasionally, the stranger's voice would drift faintly into the house.

"The explosion happened right before he showed up. Means your father had no money to give. So I'm thinking he did it to show the guy, hey, if you don't stop coming around, I'm gonna kill myself. That was the message. And he even managed to get his daughter, who never leaves the house, to go out. What timing! Bet you had no idea your father was up to all of that?"

Just as Detective Kim had said, Se-oh did not know her father. To put it precisely, the father she knew was different from the father he knew.

Her father was a man who hoisted a three-kilogram dumbbell every morning and groaned, "This is killing me!" He did it not for the exercise but to wake Se-oh, who was a heavy sleeper, with his grumbling. He claimed he did it because he hated to eat alone, but she knew it was because he worried about her skipping meals. On weekends, he sat on the sofa and watched comedy programs on TV just so he could spend time with her. Whenever she laughed, he would laugh, too, and say, "That slays me!" He didn't say that because the show was funny but because it made him happy to see his daughter smile. When news about a politician came on the screen, he would curse and say, "They should all just drop dead!" It was the obvious, meek resignation of a powerless man. When he got dust in his eye while changing the bulb in the ceiling lamp, he would loudly exaggerate the pain and say, "That could've been fatal." When he was coming home from a night of drinking and took the bus in order to save on cab fare only to fall asleep and forget his glasses on the bus, he would tell her, "Scrimping will be the death of me," and while turning a sock with a hole in it inside out in order to darn it, he would brag, "How's that? Skills to die for, right?" He also used to brag about the fact that, back when their house was built, he had stacked the bricks himself instead of hiring laborers, as if by doing so he'd single-handedly saved the nation from certain death, and would point out repeatedly patched-over cracks in cement walls and loudly mourn the shameful state of the construction industry that couldn't even build a single wall properly. If Se-oh cooked so much as a single pot of stew, he would exclaim that the flavor was "killer" and slurp noisily. Every month he bought her menstrual pads without her having to ask, and he would comment that if he kept that up he would soon "die of embarrassment." These were all the ways that Su-chang Yun, the father Se-oh Yun knew, talked about death.

Detective Kim did not know any of that. He thought there was plenty of reason for her father to be depressed: he had debt, he had a grown daughter who kept herself cooped up at home, and the store he'd owned for over ten years had been sold off for practically nothing when the shopping plaza it was in was zoned for redevelopment, which caused his debt to grow even higher. Detective Kim was right. Right to think that before the worst had happened, things were already terrible.

Se-oh agreed. It was not just one thing, but rather one thing after another and another, like links in a chain, piling the bad luck higher and higher around her father and #157, until it exploded. And Detective Kim had unwittingly revealed one of those links to Se-oh. The person who had forced her father to make an extreme choice, the person who had made her father sit all alone on the couch as the smell of gas spread around him, the person who had made him resort to a tiny insurance policy with his own life as collateral. Se-oh committed that person's name to memory.

6

Se-oh, after keeping herself shut indoors for so long, had finally left the house again when her father hurt his tailbone. It took her two and a half hours to go to the bank and back. She had to pay the utility bills not through a bank teller but at a machine that looked a lot like an ATM but was designed expressly for paying bills. It bewildered her. After a good bit of puzzling, she got the security guard's help, and as she was feeding the bill stubs into the machine, she was struck by how the world kept on changing, as it always had, quickly, indifferently, and with no regard for her.

By the time she got home, her body was trembling and feverish. But she had succeeded at something. She had thought if she so much as set foot outside, she would run into someone intent on tracking her down. That people would be lying in wait around every corner to accost her. It was not the case. It had happened to her long ago, but not anymore. There was no one hiding behind a utility pole, keeping a lookout on the alley. There were no threatening letters in her mailbox. No one had graffitied curses on the wall.

There was one person who stared. It scared her at first, but when she gave it a little thought, she realized it was probably because of the large surgical mask covering her face and the knit cap she was wearing out of season. Most everyone else walked right by without a second glance, not even at the cap. The whole time she had stayed locked up at home, she had imagined the outside world as a place that could swallow her whole at any moment. But in truth, it was a place that paid her no attention at all.

From that first outing, her father had learned the trick to getting Se-oh out of the house was for him to be bedridden, and so afterward he was frequently unwell. The less well he was, the better he was able to get her out.

It had also taught Se-oh that no one was going to recognize her and come charging after her. That said, it wasn't enough to convince herself the world was safe. She had just gotten lucky. She agreed to the next errand in order to test her luck again. This time, it was to a large grocery store. She kept her head bowed so low that she attracted the attention of an employee. Each time Se-oh bent down to look for something, the employee bent down too, and followed Se-oh as she moved along the rows. But that was as far as it went. No one tried to hunt her down or attack her.

By gradually venturing outside the house, taking her time as she went, Se-oh learned that while the world contained everything she was afraid of, it was not all going to come rushing at her at once. This was a little bit depressing. Not only was the world indifferent, she also had to wonder if the people whom she'd assumed were suffering because of her had in fact forgotten all about her. But that was impossible. They couldn't have forgotten her any more than Se-oh could have forgotten those she was connected to. That they had not yet appeared was not due to the kindness of coincidence but because they were still in hiding.

Before leaving the house, she counted the people she dared not run across. On some days, she counted more than thirty, but there were also days when she thought of only ten. But that was still more than the people she had to see or wanted to see. That gap never shrank.

The day of the accident, her father had sent her to a department store near the bus terminal.

"If you leave at two thirty, the timing will be perfect."

Unlike for her other errands, her father had set an exact time for her to leave, but Se-oh didn't ask why. If she had, would her father have finally told her what was really going on and asked her advice? Had he ever felt hurt by the fact that Se-oh was so unresponsive, never arguing with him or questioning anything?

"Be safe out there."

Her father said that to her as she was leaving. She glanced back at him. He was standing outside the front door, watching her go. When she reached the end of the alley and glanced back again, her father was still standing there. Se-oh petted the yellow dog and walked out of the alley.

When she'd arrived at the department store counter with the claim check her father had given her, the sales clerk greeted her and brought out an item wrapped in plastic.

"Why don't you try it on?"

"Excuse me?"

"Your father put so much care into picking this out for you."

She'd stared at the sales clerk, wondering if she'd heard her correctly. The clerk offered her the item again.

Clothing. That her father had picked out. Just for her. He had walked around a fancy department store and selected this item of clothing for her. For her birthday. He had never given her a gift of clothing before.

Se-oh slowly unpacked her father's actions step by step. It helped to reduce her wonder and awe and doubt. But progressing to the final step didn't come naturally. Doubt continued to linger. Questions like, why on earth did he do that?

It was a purple trench coat. The neckline was round, and the hem narrowed at the bottom like a vase. The pocket was embroidered with two cherries and a green leaf. It was girly. It was not pretty. It looked more like a tablecloth than clothing.

"Try it on. We should probably check the size," the sales clerk said. She seemed to sense that Se-oh didn't care for the coat.

Se-oh stood in front of the mirror. Just as something could be girly and still be ugly, it could also be ugly yet still look good on her. She took off her long, blue padded coat and put on the purple trench coat. There in the mirror was Se-oh Yun wearing the very first item of clothing purchased for her by her father.

He had never given her anything he had picked out himself. He might have given her some little things when she was young, but after she'd grown up, all he gave her was spending money. And after she shut herself up at home, there was no need for that either. Did he think that the daughter who never left the house would want to go out if she had something new to wear?

Her father knew Se-oh didn't have anything appropriate for the weather. He also knew that trench coats were the latest trend. But he did not know that he knew next to nothing about his own daughter.

"Shall I bring you a different size?" the clerk asked Se-oh's reflection in the mirror. The sleeves were squeezing her forearms, and the shoulder seams were hiked up close to her neck. The clerk brought out a bigger size and helped Se-oh try it on. Se-oh's father was always nagging her to eat more. Too skinny. Nothing but bones. He'd probably said the same thing to the clerk. She picks at her food. She's so skinny.

"This size is perfect. Or I could show you some pants?"

Se-oh took that to mean that while the coat fit, the clerk thought the style didn't suit her at all. She shook her head.

In the mirror stood a short woman dressed in a purple trench coat. The edges of the T-shirt that stuck out of the coat were frayed. Her unmade-up face looked dry.

The coat didn't suit her, but there was one thing she'd liked. The thickness of the fabric. It had seemed just right for the weather. Though it was still cold out, the wind was no longer biting, and so she'd thought she could get away with wearing something that thin and brightly colored. But more than anything, it was the first article of clothing her father had ever picked out for her. Of course, she didn't know at the time that it would also be the last.

7

You can pick apart a dead body all you want, but nothing will be made clear. The autopsy results said the cause of death was drowning. Plankton was found in the lungs. It wasn't clear whether it was suicide or an accidental death. The time of death was estimated to be early January, three months prior. Ki-jeong Shin listened mutely to the detective's message. Amid all the unclarity, Ki-jeong's certainty that it was suicide remained unchanged. The police seemed to think the same thing. Especially now that her sister's debts had come to light.

Her sister's debt was nearly equal to the amount Ki-jeong had saved, starting from her entry-level part-time teaching position all the way through her tenure as a full-time teacher. Ki-jeong felt discouraged. In death as in life, her little sister was a burden.

Ki-jeong was calm and composed all throughout the simple funeral she hosted on her own. Now and then she sensed that she was being too stoic. It occurred to her that what she was feeling was not normal, so she put on a performance of the emotions and facial expressions expected for the scene. She played the character of an older sister who was silent from the exhaustion of protracted grief. She had always turned to acting when she could not quite figure out what she really felt.

After the funeral was over and she returned to work, there were several more situations that required her to do some acting. Acting helped Ki-jeong to pull off the role of teacher with ease. When she wasn't sure what to say to a student who had come to her for guidance, when she doubted whether she was justified in expressing her feelings, and when she was angry because of an unruly child, she thought of herself as playing the role of a teacher in some grand experimental theater production. As long as she thought the person playing the role of student was supposed to always make mistakes and get into unexpected trouble, then her mind was more or less at ease.

Otherwise, if she didn't, she would lapse into regarding the children as overgrown insects. She found herself wanting to crush them under her foot or strike them mercilessly with something sharp. Bugs startled Ki-jeong by scurrying quickly toward her or suddenly spreading their wings and taking off, and in that respect they were no different from children. You could never predict which way children were going to move, and they were tenacious and dull in their stubbornness. After she had explained something once and asked if they understood, they said they did not. She would slowly explain again, but it made no difference. Ki-jeong would play the role of a patient teacher and repeat her explanation to the children. When she turned her back to write the identical information on the chalkboard, she could hear them snickering behind her back.

Teaching was the career her mother had most desired for her. Ki-jeong escaped her high-strung and easily irritated mother's constant meddling by willingly adopting that desire as her own.

She often based her actions on what she thought other people wanted. Because she was always busy satisfying other people's expectations, the sight of someone who easily decided what they wanted left her wallowing in inferiority.

The nature of her job demanded a sense of duty. By the time she realized it wasn't right for her, her job had already turned her into someone unsuited for any other career. Nevertheless, she did want, sometimes, to do her job properly. She just didn't know what that would take. Her students were bright, but when she pictured them growing up and becoming adults, everything felt hopeless.

She first became aware she was acting after reading about an experiment at an American university. The test subjects were divided up into pairs of "teachers" and "learners." The "learner" would solve a simple exercise in which they connected matching pairs of words, and if a mistake was made, the "teacher" would inflict corporal punishment on the incorrect "learner" with an electric shock. The purpose was to increase their ability to learn; each time they made a mistake, the shock went up ten more volts.

Ki-jeong sometimes felt like the teacher in that experiment. That is, she felt like she was compulsively performing a set role, held captive by a sense of responsibility and by orders from above.

Do-jun seemed to be the same way. Now, when others were around, whether during class or in the teachers' lounge, he was engrossed in the role of "learner." He behaved meekly, down-hearted and hesitant, as if regretting what he had done. But when it was just the two of them, he and Ki-jeong, he was different. He was confident, as if already exonerated, because Ki-jeong was his accomplice who had misappropriated stolen goods.

When she called Do-jun's parents, she felt like the experiment had started over. The person in the role of "learner's father" asked, "You're his teacher?" and raised his voice at her: "You call my boy a thief just because he stole one little pack of gum? You should be teaching him not to steal, not threatening him!" He added: "I hear you took the stolen goods for yourself. Seems to me if my kid's a thief, then so are you. You should both go to jail." And threatened: "If my kid has to sit in detention in the counselor's office, then you'll be sitting at home without a job." Then he said, in mock politeness: "I'm going to go check out these stolen goods, so let's meet in the trustees office, shall we? We'll see what the chairman thinks about you messing with his customers." Ki-jeong imagined that someone in charge of the experiment was watching and that she had to bring this part of the experiment to a successful close, and so she suffered it patiently.

It was strange that it looked like the same experiment up till now. That is, an experiment confirming submission to authority. Ki-jeong would tolerate it for a while before angrily wondering why this had happened to her. Then, in the end, she would regret her mistakes and apologize to anyone and everyone.

"It's okay. He'll get suspended. Hold on a little longer."

When Trig said that to console her, she was still thinking about the experiment.

She continued thinking about it the whole way back to the teachers' lounge after class. When she passed the counselor's office, the door of which stood open, she saw Do-jun sitting arrogantly with his feet propped on the desk, and all at once she remembered: The "teacher" had used his authority to violently discipline the "learner." As the experiment progressed, the "learner" received electric shocks while begging to quit. The "teacher," trapped by the responsibility to complete the experiment, considered it only reasonable to exert control over the "learner" and administer stronger and stronger electric shocks.

The gist of the experiment was to warn people that, when placed in a position of authority, an individual's ability to think critically and autonomously shrinks. It demonstrated that, when an inflexible authority confronts the moral value that says do no harm, in most cases the authority wins.

Do-jun Weon stared at Ki-jeong through the open door. The boy flashed a grin. He bobbed his head as if gesturing for her to come on in. Do-jun gave no thought to taking his feet off of the desk; he looked entirely too comfortable for a student on probation. That was the only disciplinary action Ki-jeong had managed to talk the vice principal into; she'd strongly opposed his suggestion that they put off dealing with Do-jun until the ringleader had emerged and the details were revealed.

Ki-jeong glowered coldly at Do-jun. He stared right back at her, not looking the slightest bit defeated. Was it the way he looked at her? Or was she once again just doing what someone expected of her? Ki-jeong entered the counselor's office and locked the door behind her with a loud click. Do-jun slipped his legs off of the desk and sat up straight. Ki-jeong took off her slipper. It was the stolen slipper Do-jun had given her. She clutched it in her right hand and brought it down with all of her strength on the boy. Do-jun let out a yelp. He curled up like a bug to avoid the next blow. But the moment Ki-jeong stopped, he lifted his head and stared at her with eyes that seemed to flash and say, Go on, hit me again. She had no doubt that was what they said.

Later, she realized it. The part she'd failed to remember at the time. The truth was that the "learners" were not being shocked at all; they were only pretending to be in pain. The "learners" were all professional actors.

Do-jun had planned on getting hit. The principal had strictly banned corporal punishment, and Do-jun knew that the teachers all knew this. Do-jun's probation would be lifted, and Ki-jeong would be punished instead. After all, the person who had pushed for a strong punishment was her and her alone.

8

As darkness spread and lights flickered on one after the other, the ruin of #157 revealed itself: the blown-out walls and incinerated kitchen, the half-obliterated armoire, the chest of drawers burnt beyond recognition, the caved-in living room ceiling, the melted lump of a cassette deck, the fallen kitchen counter, the dining table collapsed on its burnt legs, the sofa reduced to its metal frame and burnt springs.

The only undamaged thing visible from the living room were the trees in the yard. Flowers had come into full bloom in the blackened earth and endured a crestfallen spring before wilting. Now, tender green leaves sprouted in their place. The dried and yellowed petals lying on the ground were quiet proof of how much time had passed.

There should have been an out-of-style chandelier hanging from the ceiling, its dim light straining to escape a thick layer of dust. There should have been a sofa against the wall to the right, the leather worn and the yellow stuffing poking through. The wall to the left should have had a long console with a boxy television set sitting on top. Now it was all gone.

In contrast, Se-oh's room was relatively unscathed. The ceramic angel music box was still in its usual spot on the bookshelf, unmarred by even the slightest trace of ash. The angel's gray eyes cast a benevolent gaze on Se-oh. She turned it so it was facing away. Having her father look at her like that was enough.

If that person on the stretcher really was my father, Se-oh had thought upon arriving at the hospital, then at least he was able to move with each tilt of the stretcher. He could wave his hand to signal that he needed help, and groan to request medical attention.

Her father had lain in the hospital bed wrapped in bandages from head to toe. It had given her a sliver of hope that maybe this wasn't really her father after all. The only proof that it was him was the name written on the chart at the foot of the bed.

Se-oh was summoned by the doctor as Su-chang Yun's legal guardian. The doctor sounded impatient and unfriendly each time he spoke, and he used too much medical jargon, the vast majority of which she couldn't understand. But she had no trouble understanding that her father was in critical condition, that treatment was difficult, and that he was very likely to die. Even without the doctor's brusque explanation, the full-body bandages and the fleet of medical equipment attached to him left her in despair.

The hospital was hot, and the hospital room was even hotter, but Se-oh had kept her purple trench coat on and refused to sit down the whole time she was there, just in case her father opened his eyes and looked up at her. She wanted him to see her wearing the coat he'd bought for her. Based on what the doctor had said, the odds were high he would never get to see it for himself and, sure enough, that was what happened.

The first morning after his funeral was silent. There was no grunting as her father hoisted his dumbbells, no grumbling as he read the newspaper, no rattling of the pressure cooker valve to signal that the rice was done, none of his usual belches upon finishing his breakfast, and no audible gulps that followed when he noticed Se-oh's frown and struggled to squelch any more burps from escaping. Her father feared Se-oh above all others. He wanted to stay on her good side. He loved her more than anyone.

No matter how she looked back at them now, Se-oh knew that those mornings and nights, days and nights, nights and nights filled with those sounds had been monotonous and dull. And yet, those same sounds struck her now as beautiful. The clanking of dumbbells, the crackling of pork on the grill, even her father's belches. Se-oh, pour me some water. Se-oh, let's eat. Se-oh, let's clean. Se-oh, aren't you going to watch TV? Se-oh, open the window. Se-oh, let's fold the laundry. Those short, simple sentences had become the most beautiful in the world.

Those sounds and sentences were lost to her now. His unconditional love, his wordless yet tender gaze, his steely look of fatherly responsibility. All gone. They were each different, but to her they were all synonyms for a father. The life filled with such things had moved on. It had become one she could only miss.

As the days spent alone increased and the night chill subsided, she began thinking about her father less. Except, of course, when she saw the purple trench coat hanging on the wall like a framed picture, or when she passed a man on the street who was of similar age as her father, or when she woke in the morning to the absence of dumbbells, or when she went to bed at night without saying good night, or when she smelled pork marinated in gochujang, or when she saw a large dog, or when she saw the scuffed, round toes of shoes in the street, or when she dropped by the burned remains of #157. In other words, other than most of the time, she did not think of him.

She was doing relatively okay. It bewildered her at times that she could go on living after losing her father and her home. While staying in the hospital with her bandaged father, she had still gotten hungry at mealtimes. She had eaten in the hospital cafeteria every day. At first it had felt like she was just stuffing herself without even tasting the food. But when she began to realize that the food itself simply had no flavor, she resented her intestines for their powers of rapid digestion. Sometimes, she took breaks from sitting beside her father to watch TV in the waiting room only to catch herself laughing at whatever was on. When an elderly woman watching the same show asked, "What did they just say?" Se-oh had repeated the line back to her.

She tried to stay in the house at first. She slept on a thick blanket that she spread on a piece of plywood but was shocked to discover that it hurt her back and left her unable to sleep. Even at a time like that, her body could still register discomfort. In the morning, her face was black with ash that had fallen from the ceiling. She washed her face thoroughly with cold water and put on a thick layer of moisturizing cream. It helped to calm her anger and her sadness, albeit temporarily.

Se-oh sat on the waterlogged floor and stared at the blackened sofa. She pictured her father's final moments. Sitting quietly on the sofa, his face stoic, waiting too long for someone to come, until he was unable to get himself to safety. Debating whether to call for help, only to give up and tell himself that it would make no difference. Watching as the house turned black and fell around him, as he thought about his daughter.

Who had put him through that? She thought about the faceless voice she'd sometimes heard outside the front door. The man who had threatened her father, made him feel his life was worthless, made him fear life, pushed him further into debt, and drove him to walk into the arms of death.

Now, with everything gone, she wasn't sure why she kept thinking about the debt collector or why it felt so important to find out who he was. Clueless as to his identity, she thought about him through the cold, dark nights that had grown so familiar. She thought about him in dreams that unspooled with no end. She thought about him night after night spent lying on the floor. She thought about him as the pea-green shoots on the tree branches turned to deep green leaves. She thought about how he had pressured her father and threatened him and terrorized him and turned everything to ruin.

Daytime Se-oh regarded those nighttime thoughts as wrong. Even with everything so unclear, that at least she was sure of. Nighttime Se-oh was stupid. So stupid that she tried to rest her crude, worthless heart on the things she'd lost.

Daytime Se-oh thought her nighttime self was awful. But she soon realized something. The only worthwhile part of her life was the time that she'd spent at home with her father.

Daytime Se-oh, to say nothing of nighttime Se-oh, knew just how stupid and awful she was. Did that man know he was no better? Or had he looked down on her father as worthless without realizing he was worthless, too? The thought of it made her so angry that it brought tears to her eyes. Her rage was indescribable. The reason for it was simple. She had nothing left in this world to love.

Se-oh packed the items that remained at #157 in a cardboard box. Her father's shoes with the rounded toes. It was fortunate they'd survived. His clothes were useless. The moment she laundered them, they would lose his scent and shape. But his shoes held the memory of his feet. She packed the reading glasses he had worn whenever he read the newspaper or checked his credit card statements. They were half-melted in their case. She packed her father's dental floss and his special toothpaste for treating his gums. She packed the music box and the letters and the few books that had survived the flood of fire hoses. Anything at least partially intact was added until the box was full.

She was taking a last look around when she spotted something sticking out from under the scorched cupboard. A claw hammer. The head was about the size of her fist, one end snub-nosed and the other curving into two broad forks. It appeared to have survived the fire by hiding under the cupboard. The end of the handle was charred, but once the ash was brushed off, it was still serviceable. The wooden handle felt agreeably warm. Perhaps in some deep, fathomless core, an ember was still burning. In stark contrast to the handle's warmth, the steel head was cold.

She squeezed the hammer tight. Her father had used it to hang the calendar on the wall. He had also used it the first time Se-oh brought home an award. He'd framed the award and hung it next to the calendar using that hammer. If she had managed to graduate, he probably would have used it again to hang a photo of her in cap and gown.

The air felt like rain. A damp breeze stirred the ashes. She carried the box out of the house and slowly turned to look back at it. This place contained the past. All of which had burned. The many days of the future that had not yet come were here also. They, too, had burned.

This parting was not particularly painful. The burned and

blackened things and the smell, as if the fire were still burning, overwhelmed Se-oh's memories. It made it easy for her to brush off the compassion, honor, generosity, and other high-minded ideas that had dwelled in that house. She sensed that the days of disappointment and suffering and anger, followed by feeling nothing at all, only to once again be brought to the verge of tears, would go on and on. They would parade by, numberless and identical. The future was a dark corridor. And though she would grope her way through it, the door at the end would be locked tight.

Se-oh carried her heavy box into that dark corridor. The alleyways that she'd always taken before were as dark and narrow and silent as her future. It felt heartless. There'd been quiet nights before. Nights when no children cried next door, when the noises of everyday life did not come from the crowded flats across the street. Late nights when no dogs barked or cars drove past or televisions blared. The silence now was thicker and denser than those nights.

While staying alone at #157, Se-oh had taken care to enter without anyone seeing her, to pass the nights with no light, to leave before it grew bright, and to return after it was dark. She did not cross paths with anyone. She'd been sure that none of her neighbors knew she was staying there.

But the silence now told her she'd been mistaken. It was a determined silence. It left her feeling convinced that they'd known all along that #157 was occupied. After all, no one had used it as their garbage dump. They'd collected the mail and stacked it neatly inside the entryway. They'd placed rocks on top to keep it from blowing away and covered it to keep the rain off. There weren't even any signs of children having snuck in to play in the door-less, wall-less house.

That thought made Se-oh stop and look back. She'd been accepting of everything while packing up their belongings, but standing there in the narrow alleyway, receiving her neighbors' silent send-off, she suddenly felt staggered by it all.

The night was moving slowly. Se-oh resumed walking. Soon she was at the end of the alley. She put down the box and sat next to the sleeping dog to stroke its head. The dog woke and looked up at her sweetly.

When she stood and picked up the box again, she realized it wasn't that heavy after all. She felt like she was finally grown. It wasn't until much later when she looked back that she realized it wasn't she who had grown that night. It was the anger pent up inside her, which had sprouted big and tall. But even knowing that didn't change her belief that she'd become an adult that night.

9

The principal sat at his desk, the look on his face saying he was sick of doing paperwork. But to Ki-jeong's surprise, there was no Do-jun posing contritely, his head hanging low in pretend shame, nor even one of his parents rushing into the office to plead with them to go easy on him or simply to make her life hell. How strange—for those who'd given her so much trouble to be so quiet now.

The principal was short but solidly built, his movements somehow heavy-looking, as if he were carrying a stack of bricks on each shoulder. He sighed frequently. It was the same no matter what he was doing—whether delivering a formal address or scolding teachers or bestowing certificates of merit on students up on stage. Ki-jeong wondered if he knew this about himself.

"Still busy with grading?" the principal asked abruptly, without inviting Ki-jeong to sit down first. He didn't look like he was expecting an actual response.

Ki-jeong shifted from foot to foot and said no.

"That's good."

The principal stood up from his desk and walked over to the

sofa, gesturing for Ki-jeong to sit with him. The sofa was large and plush; if you weren't careful, you could end up looking too comfortable sitting on it. Ki-jeong perched right on the edge and wondered what could possibly be good about not being busy.

The principal stared at her for a moment without saying anything. Ki-jeong kept quiet, too. She was always at a loss for what to say whenever she found herself alone with the principal. He was always so silent and would merely stare at her, as if waiting for her to say something first. Then he'd let out another sigh. When she finally did manage to drag something out of her mouth, he never paid attention, forcing her to repeat the same words over and over. Then he'd point out the mistakes in what she'd said or respond as if she hadn't told him anything he didn't already know. Talking to him always left her feeling deflated.

A chorus of laughter arose from a group of children cleaning up the flowerbed outside the window. One of them said something loudly, and a volley of noise followed. The principal's office grew chillier and more uncomfortable. He started to get up from the couch. Ki-jeong assumed he was going to close the window, so she jumped up first and closed it for him. He let out a small sigh.

When she sat back down, the principal slid an envelope toward her. He said nothing, but his demeanor demanded that she take a good look at it.

Inside were two sheets of paper. One contained a list of items that could be purchased at a stationery store or grocery store. Ki-jeong immediately guessed what it was and confirmed her guess when she saw the word "slippers" included there. The other was a doctor's certificate showing that Do-jun had been hospitalized. Ki-jeong had to hold back her nausea when she saw it.

The principal muttered something that Ki-jeong couldn't quite make out. But despite his slurring of the words "bribery" and "assault," she got the gist of it.

He pointed to her slippers and said, "I presume those are the offending objects?" He followed with another sigh. She wasn't sure if the offense referred to the fact that the slippers were stolen goods or that she'd hit a child with them. The principal said nothing more but simply gazed at Ki-jeong for a moment longer and returned to his desk.

Ki-jeong stayed put on the sofa. It wasn't fair. She wished she could get her thoughts in order and argue with him. He kept on sighing and sniffing through what sounded like a congested nose. He didn't tell her to leave, and she made no move to do so.

The minutes ticked by. The principal picked up his phone. After a moment, he said, "Yes, it's me. Could you come here? It's regarding the substitute homeroom teacher for Room 6." Finally, Ki-jeong stood and slowly shuffled out of the office, letting the stolen slippers that Do-jun had given her drag across the floor.

As soon as she stepped into the teachers' lounge, a group of teachers who'd been huddled together and talking went silent all at once and hurried back to their seats. Clearly, word had gotten out. Ki-jeong's hands shook; she tried to pull her bag out from under her desk but dropped it instead. Trig picked up the items strewn across the floor. Ki-jeong tried to smile at him.

Failure. Her face was too frozen in place to smile. Any thought she'd had of playing it cool flew out the window, along with her determination to show that she could handle anything, even an injustice like this.

Trig stared at her as he handed her things back. If the guidance counselor and the closed-circuit camera that recorded everything were what had revealed that she'd mercilessly beat a student, then was Trig the one who had told everyone she'd been taking bribes from Do-jun? Hadn't she wanted to show off to her fellow teachers, to brag about how popular she was among the students while sharing with them the gifts Do-jun had given her? Maybe Trig had caught on to her vanity.

Didn't they see how unfair it was? Ki-jeong muttered inwardly at her fellow teachers as they pretended to be busily absorbed in their work. Wasn't it too steep a price to pay, even for vanity? And yet, at the same time, she realized that the true source of her anger was not Do-jun. Her anger arose from a much deeper place. Mixed up with it was the repugnance she felt toward the principal and vice principal who were under the thumb of the chairman of the board, the alienation she felt at being among fellow teachers who would only socialize with those who'd graduated from the same college as them, and something else, something bordering on contempt for Do-jun's parents.

Her face stony, she slowly shouldered her bag and walked out of the building. The students working on the grounds outside opened a path for her, stealing glances as she passed and regrouping to chatter in her wake. She ignored the ever-friendly security guard as he chirped, "Clocking out early today!"

On the bus ride home, her phone rang. It was the police. Only then did she realize she'd boarded the bus on the wrong side of the street and was headed away from home. The phone stopped ringing. She got off at the next stop. As she thought about what the cops might tell her, her anger subsided.

The officer gave her the name and address of the person who'd made the last call to her sister's phone. As usual, they'd been unable to get in contact with that person. Ki-jeong put up with the officer's incompetence; she lacked the energy today to get angry with him. She didn't recognize the name. Just as she hadn't recognized anything else having to do with her sister's case. Ki-jeong said nothing. The officer added a few more details. The person was around the same age as her sister.

Ki-jeong instantly committed the name to memory. She'd never heard that name before, and yet it now seemed as familiar as that of an old friend.

10

David Credit Information Company was located in the E— Building at the northern end of Mapo Bridge. The twenty-five-story building had three entrances: one door in front, one to the left that opened on to a park, and one to the right that opened on to a sidewalk. According to the directory in the first-floor lobby, the building housed a total of thirty-two businesses: the first and second floors were occupied by a bank while the third through eighth floors were mostly medical clinics, which meant that the building got a large number of visitors throughout the day. David Credit took up the entire seventeenth floor and had a security system that prevented anyone but employees from entering any part of it except for the customer service department.

A little past eight thirty in the morning, the subway station exit was crowded with people on their way to work. Su-ho Lee appeared right on schedule. He never headed up to the office right away but instead would pop into a food place next door to buy some kimbap or grab a snack from the convenience store in front of the park. Judging by the fact that he ate breakfast on the go every day, Se-oh had assumed at first that he lived alone. But now she knew most people grabbed breakfast on the go. She decided against jumping to any hasty conclusions whatsoever when it came to Su-ho Lee. Thinking she knew anything for certain was likely to cause her trouble.

Her goal was to learn as much as she could about him. She would collect data, compile statistics, extract probabilities. She would turn him into a subject from which assumptions and predictions could be safely drawn. She wanted her plan to succeed. That was what sustained Se-oh in the present, in which her past was lost to her entirely and her inner self had completely vanished.

She kept losing him at lunchtime. It was impossible to keep her eye on all three entrances at the same time, and she couldn't just stalk every single man dressed like him on the off-chance that it would be Su-ho. In fact, there was always the possibility of him not coming out of the building at all. There were several restaurants down on the first basement floor.

He usually went to lunch alone; other times he was in a group of up to four people. They appeared to be always the same people. He never met anyone separately for lunch. As a group, they usually went out for hangover soup, and on hot days they ate cold noodles.

Whenever she missed him on his way out to a restaurant, she waited in the park. Twice a week or so, he would stop by a convenience store after lunch and then head there. Usually, he bought cigarettes and coffee or yogurt.

To one side of the park was playground equipment, including a slide and a seesaw; to the other was some simple exercise equipment. There were plenty of benches, too. Su-ho always sat on the side of the park with the exercise equipment, where he would chain-smoke for the remainder of his lunch break before returning to the office via the entrance closest to the sidewalk. Around 2:00 p.m., he would reappear at the building's front entrance and head out somewhere. That was when his real work began in earnest.

She joined him on his subway rides, through every transfer. She seldom got lucky enough to be able to follow him to the end. It was so easy to lose him. He walked fast. And there were many days when she couldn't find a good hiding spot from which to keep an eye on him. She'd lose him while trying to avoid being spotted by him on his way back.

Each time she found herself wandering through yet another unfamiliar neighborhood and braving the afternoon heat in order to tail Su-ho, she wondered where this had all begun. Not that everything necessarily had to have a beginning and an end. But Se-oh was sure that there must have been some clear starting point. A single point that had determined everything. A point of divergence from everything that had come before. A point in time that she could look back on after much more time had passed and say that that was the point from which everything had changed.

Was it the moment she'd heard the name Su-ho Lee? As soon as she heard Detective Kim say his name, Se-oh had immediately inferred that Su-ho was responsible for the explosion at #157. Once the thought was in her head, no other hypotheses would present themselves.

While tailing Su-ho, she thought mostly about her father. She thought a little about herself, too. She'd thought she'd known her father well. She'd believed that he would never have made the choice he'd been accused of making. She'd had no reason to think otherwise. She had been confident in what she believed.

But no longer. She was beginning to understand that the life she'd known up until now was an uncertain thing, always abruptly halting or changing direction and sliding toward parts unknown.

Since there was a starting point, there also had to be an end point. In other words, there was now a future that could not be predicted. She had no idea whether it would leave her happy or sad. Life would run its course regardless, with some purpose or resolution, determination or will to action. It was better than being stagnant.

In the meantime, Se-oh had pictured what Su-ho would look and sound like, had imagined his school background, his hobbies, his family and friends. She'd thought about him so much that when she finally did lay eyes on him for the first time, she was certain she had the wrong person. The Su-ho that she'd imagined had broad shoulders, a well-defined chest, forearms that bulged with muscles below his rolled-up sleeves, large, thick hands that could palm a basketball, black hair, and a tanned face.

But the real Su-ho Lee was not large or intimidating or menacing. He wasn't even tall enough to tower over anyone. No one would feel scared crossing paths with him. He spit a lot, but he came off as more scruffy than criminal. He didn't swagger around giving people the hairy eyeball, or size everyone and everything up with daggers in his eyes. He didn't wear his hair in a militant crewcut. He didn't pair suits with T-shirts and sneakers. His eyes were neither shifty nor bulging. His voice was not gravelly.

He stood maybe five eight at most. He always wore black shoes. The soles must have been made of some soft material, as they made no sound as he walked. He was small-framed and skinny. He wore plastic-framed glasses that were a different color on the inside rim than the outside, and he was habitually pushing them back up his nose. Whenever he talked to his coworkers, he spoke slowly and let his sentences trail off.

He alternated between two suits. Both pairs of pants were so loose on him that the legs looked empty. But not because he was too skinny; the pants were simply the wrong size. The jacket shoulders extended far past his actual shoulders in an outdated style no longer sold in stores. Perhaps he had lost weight very suddenly and hadn't yet had the chance to have the pants or jacket taken in. He rarely bothered to adjust his clothes after shouldering his bag, so one side of his jacket was usually hitched up all the way to his waist. He wore a loud tie, too, which made him look old and like a hick.

Up close, he smelled faintly of sweat and cigarettes. Emerging from the subway station in the mornings, his hair would look relatively well-combed only to end up disheveled and greasy by afternoon. The dandruff on his jacket was visible. Overdue for a trim, the hair at the back of his head curled up in a slight ducktail. He looked tired, worn down.

But contrary to his air of virtuous exhaustion, Su-ho Lee was not a good person. To put a finer point on it, he was tired because he was not good. He tormented others relentlessly, assailing them with words chosen to coerce and annoy. He badgered them so much to pay off their debts, it seemed as if he were taking revenge for having an unrewarding job. He demanded that they take responsibility while laying claim to their property, and threatened them by casually mentioning the names of their loved ones. He mocked people who'd labored their whole lives with no respite only to be left with nothing but debt. And in so doing, he filled them with resentment toward their families who couldn't help, or left them feeling remorse for becoming a burden. He made them hate the simple, earnest lives they'd once led.

But perhaps it wasn't the fault of his disposition or temperament; he didn't act purely of his own volition or react according to his mood. Most likely he was obeying the strictures of his job, his training, or the general attitude of the company, which emphasized the efficient carrying out of business above all else. That had to be it. Or else he'd deluded himself into thinking that terrorizing your targets through sarcasm and mockery and blame and profanity would improve his collection rate.

But even so, the things a person said and did had a way of ruining them little by little. Whoever he was in the beginning, Su-ho Lee had long since been corrupted. He did not choose his words or shape his actions to meet the demands of his job; rather, the job he'd found suited him.

Detective Kim had suggested that human beings weren't inherently evil. That they were capable of being honest and well-intentioned and putting others first. Despite the terrible things that happened in the world and the uncertainty of it all, one of the few truths was that, deep down, people were good. But knowing that made no difference to a mind made up. To take action, Se-oh would have to ignore the truth. Because, above all, people are always doing what they said they "would never" do. Because hitting people, lying to them, toying with them, conning them out of their money, threatening them until they thought they were better off dead? That was also what people did.

11

Whenever he found himself on the subway staring vacantly out the window opposite him, Su-ho Lee thought back to the time he'd sat next to the team leader on the subway, after his first assignment outside the office. Su-ho had broken into a cold sweat. The team leader wordlessly handed him a handkerchief. A freshly pressed, checkered handkerchief. It suited the man, who looked like he belonged in the financial district, like a stockbroker, maybe, or an executive at an IT company.

Su-ho had accepted the handkerchief with trembling hands, pretended to dab his forehead with it, then handed it back. The team leader had laughed quietly as he took the still-pristine hand-kerchief. Su-ho stealthily studied their reflection in the window. A long shadow passed lengthwise over the other man's face.

"Are you afraid of me right now?" the team leader had asked, aiming the question at Su-ho's reflection.

"Uh, no, sir."

That was a lie. He was very afraid. And envious. Su-ho wished he had the same power as this man. The power to slay someone with a single word, to beat someone with only a look, to make your opponent wither at nothing more than the sound of your breath.

The team leader turned to him. Su-ho kept looking straight ahead.

"Listen. If you're going to do this work, there are two things you absolutely cannot spill. Do you know what those are?"

Su-ho lowered his head. He didn't dare look the team leader in the eye or his entire body might have started to shake uncontrollably.

"Why won't you look at me, you little shit? Scared?" The man's mouth barely opened as he spoke. It looked like he was throwing his voice.

"No, sir."

"Then answer me. And if you say tears, you're dead. There's nothing wrong with a man spilling tears. If he wants to cry, he should go ahead and cry. Why knock yourself out trying to hold back your tears?"

He spoke through clenched teeth, just as he had with the debtor they'd gone to accost moments before. Su-ho had been about to say "tears," but he quickly changed his answer.

"Sp-spit, sir."

"Spit, huh? All right, I'll give you points for creativity. What's the other thing you shouldn't spill?"

"R-r-rice."

"R-r-r-rice?" The team leader laughed. "It's fucking hilarious watching you stutter."

Su-ho stared at the window, wondering whether or not he should laugh, too. The team leader laughed with a grimace. It looked a lot like crying.

"It's not unusual to spit a little when you're talking. You going to quit your job over a little spit? As for rice, remember that DJ Doc song? It went something like, 'Do you have to be good at using chopsticks in order to eat? You can still eat plenty even if you're bad at it.' I guess from now on you better not drop a single grain of rice when you're eating with me. If you do, you're dead."

"Yes, sir."

"'Yes, sir?' That's not how real men talk. What'll become of you at this rate? There's a fine line between having a positive attitude and groveling. Knock it off."

"Yes, sir."

"Listen: the answer is sweat and piss. Spilling those are worse than getting your ass kicked by some clown with no money. And you've already spilled some sweat. If you piss yourself, you're done. Got it? So keep that in mind. You've already spilled one. Don't fuck up again."

Su-ho clenched the muscles in his groin. The team leader laughed and turned to stare at a girl sitting across from them.

From that day on, the team leader's warning haunted Su-ho. He'd meant that Su-ho had only one shot left. Since Su-ho had already let his team leader see him sweat, he'd have to do whatever it took to keep from pissing himself. He'd have to guard his piss with his life. Guarding your piss . . . What a joke. And yet, the more he obsessed over it, the more he knew that that was his sole task.

They had nearly reached their stop before the team leader spoke again.

"Do you know why our company is called David?"

"N-n-no, sir."

"For fuck's sake, where's your company loyalty? You *do* know the story of David and Goliath, at least, right?"

"Yes, sir."

"What's it about?"

"Uh . . . David beats Goliath?"

"That's all you've got to say? What'd you do, go to school in China? What's the *moral* of the story?"

"Uhh . . . that no matter how weak you are, as long as you use your head, you can beat a giant . . . or something like that."

"We're David, and the debtors we're collecting from are Goliath. David doesn't fight Goliath empty-handed. He takes rocks with him. He throws one at Goliath and hits him in exactly the right spot. Goliath falls. Then David rushes in, grabs his knife, and stabs him. The end."

"Aren't w-we Goliath?"

"Why would I bother saying something so clichéd? Look, you know how on a contract, there's Party A who sets the terms, and Party B who follows them? Party A is whoever has something to give, whereas Party B is the one who receives. And he who has something to give has all the power. Debtors give us money, which clearly makes them Party A. They hold the power. They're like the boss who writes your paycheck, see? You've noticed that debtors, those fuckers, never want to give us the time of day? That's how it always is with Party A. What makes it worse is that they have no actual money, which gives them balls of steel. They're fearless. And what've we got? Nothing but paper. We need stones, five of them, just like David, if we're going to take them down."

"Stones?"

"Yes, goddammit, stones. It hurts to get hit by a stone. But what I really mean is we've got to cuss Goliath out, threaten him, never let him rest. Understand? When we cuss at someone, we're not just throwing words, we're throwing stones. The people we collect from are Goliath. They're Party A. And we've got the rocks to take them down."

"Yes, sir."

"What, then, is the knife we use to chop off Goliath's head?"

"M-m-money."

"Dumbass, money is what they spill after we knife them. For god's sake, use your brain! A knife. Something lethal. Something that kills in an instant. What might that be? Family, of course! When you reach the point where you know it's time to slip the blade between their ribs, you oh so casually mention their family. That's why it's important to find out all that stuff about them beforehand."

Knife. Lethal. Kills in an instant. As Su-ho thought back now on the team leader's advice, his mouth filled with saliva.

He spat it onto the ground the moment he was off the train. No sooner had he started concentrating on not spilling any more sweat or piss than he was already getting into the habit of shedding his other bodily fluids. He looked around. A heavyset woman walking down the sidewalk gave him the side-eye; she must've seen him spit. He rubbed the saliva into the ground with the sole of his shoe, then lit a cigarette and headed off through the shopping district with its gauntlet of neon signs, straight toward Gojan-dong.

His criteria for selecting a job had been simple. It had to be a place where he could wear a suit and be at work by 9:00 a.m. every day. That was all. His father, a manual laborer who'd been dead a long time now, had always had to check the weather before heading out to work. As long as it wasn't that, Su-ho was fine with any type of job.

He'd gotten lucky. He'd been unemployed for several years

after finishing his military service, until one day he got a call from one of his army buddies. At the barbecue joint in Mapo where they met, his friend showed up in a business suit. He fit right in on that neon-lit street crowded with high-rises and noisy with cars racing endlessly toward Mapo Bridge and the Gangbyeon Expressway.

With his suit wrinkled just so, his necktie loosened, and the sleeves of his white button-down rolled up to his elbows as he brought pieces of undercooked pork ribs to his mouth and downed shots of soju, Su-ho's army buddy had looked unbearably cool. The place had been packed with other office workers who looked just like him. Every one of them was audibly cussing about someone, the air filled with "fucks" and "goddamns" and "sons of bitches." He'd envied them. The only person Su-ho had to cuss about was his own inept self.

In the army, his friend had been teased and called a girl. He was shy and timid, and each time he got a dressing down from a superior officer he would run to the bathroom and weep until his eyes were bloodshot. "You'd be a good fit," he said to Su-ho between bites of pork. "Maybe *really* good." Su-ho had thought to himself, *If this jackass can do it, then of course I'll be a lot better at it.*

How happy he'd been when he passed the interview with flying colors. Considering how most of the luck that had rolled his way so far in life had been bad luck, landing a job at a company in a twenty-five-story office building in Mapo where he got to wear a suit and report to work every morning at 9:00 a.m. sharp was just about the best luck he'd ever had.

And that was where his luck had ended. Given his shit resume, it was hardly surprising. He'd had his doubts when they threw him straight into work without any training, but it did not sway his faith in the suit. A business suit would never steer anyone wrong. When he found out that his job required him to routinely deploy verbal abuse, intimidation, mockery, and scorn, and when he witnessed the team leader doing the same, he did his best to hide his fear.

Right up until their first house call, with the team leader ringing the doorbell as gently as a church elder who'd come to spread the gospel, Su-ho's hopes had not yet faded. He still clung to the idea that his job would consist of nothing more than politely shaking hands with the debtor, giving them their letter of notification, pointing out the part about fulfillment of payment, and finalizing it all on paper.

Afterward, he'd met his friend again. He was righteously pissed but didn't know who he should get angry at. *So this is why office workers do nothing but bitch about their jobs the moment they get together*, he'd thought. He was ready to confront his friend and ask, How low do you think of me that you'd recommend me for *this* job? I'd be *really* good at it, you say? His new job was more crooked than being in the Mob.

"What? It suits you," his friend had said with a smirk. His shirt was badly wrinkled. It looked like someone had grabbed him by the front of it.

"How so?"

"You really don't know?"

"How the fuck does it suit me?"

"Think about it."

"Think about what?"

"The pricks with good luck all do well at it. It's like that proverb: Seventy percent luck, thirty percent effort. That's you."

"You son of a bitch, what the fuck do you know? I have the worst luck in the world."

His friend had stared at him for a moment and then broke into a grin. Su-ho knew that look well. He'd seen it before. If not on his friend's face, then on his own. The look that said, Think again.

He remembered something. Back in the army, their foul-tempered senior officer used to punish them by rolling him and his similarly-sized friend up in blankets and ordering the other recruits to switch them around and mix them up like pieces on a game board. Then the officer would choose one of them at random for a beating. The officer claimed it would be unfair to select one of them on purpose, and that by doing it randomly, whoever got beat was simply unlucky. Every single time, Su-ho's friend was the one picked. Seventy percent luck, thirty percent effort. That was what their officer used to say right before beating him.

Each time his friend had exploded into anger, Su-ho had mocked him and called him a luckless bastard. It was partly to hide his own remorse. Luck was the reward for Su-ho's efforts. In order to secure his luck, Su-ho had done anything and everything he could for their superior officer behind his friend's back.

He'd been born into this world with nothing, and so it made sense to cover his own ass at all times. While his friend relied on luck, Su-ho learned to make his own luck. He'd thought his friend didn't know anything about it, but maybe, Su-ho thought, his friend had known all along.

"Try to hold out for three months," his friend said, switching to a cajoling tone. "It's called the devil's triangle—if you can suffer through the first three months, you'll make it three years, and then, just like that, thirty years will have passed. It works better if you tell yourself that it's your money they borrowed."

"But it's *not* my money, so how could I? You've got a fucked-up way of encouraging a person."

Su-ho jeered, but his friend's advice did the trick: he understood at once the gist of the job. He had to be tenacious, and cruel. He had to tell himself he was only getting back what he'd loaned.

The cold sweat he'd shed that first day turned out to be an important lesson. He did as the team leader had taught him. If he was able to make his own luck back in his army days, then there was no reason he couldn't do the same now. He showed up at people's homes unannounced, surprising his targets, interfered with their daily lives within legal limits, and casually let it be known what he was doing there. He refused to smile, raised his eyebrows often, bared his teeth. Now and then he spoke gently, smiled warmly, and casually mentioned the names and information of their family members, which he'd acquired illegally.

It did not take him long. The realization that he wasn't just okay at his job but was actually very good at it filled him with self-loathing. But that, too, was momentary. Just as the team leader had said, scorn and mockery, intimidation and verbal attacks were David's stones. Like a lumberjack chopping down perfectly good trees in order to thin the forest, Su-ho chipped away at himself, readily, for the sake of money.

As his friend said, it was easier once he thought of it as having loaned his own money to the debtors. It wasn't inaccurate, either. If he didn't collect, then he didn't get a paycheck. But that didn't mean all he did was harass people. Depending on their circumstances, he might give them a month or two. Sometimes he smiled and said things like, "We have to help each other out. Isn't that what being a human being is all about?" He only said that to those from whom he might salvage something. When he gave them a second chance, those once-frightened people readily trusted him.

They consulted with him about how they might pay down their debt. They wanted to try. They thought of him as a good person.

Once he had something to collect, however little, his attitude changed at once. He became merciless. People in debt could not rely on anyone and had to be ready to flee at a moment's notice.

Even while missing each and every one of their due dates, the debtors all grumbled about unfairness and said the same thing: "Money lies, not people." But that wasn't true. People were liars. They scoffed at credit. They never once kept their promises to pay off their debts or to meet their due dates. They didn't give a second thought to taking out loans, and when the time came to pay them off, they blamed their creditors for not considering the unpredictability of time.

They used other people's money and had the nerve to yell, "You think you can treat me this way just because I have no money?" When Su-ho quietly responded, "Yes, I do," they shouted, "You think you have the right? You scum!" To which Su-ho responded simply, "That's right, I am scum."

It was the same with Ki-in Ku, who lived in Gojan-dong. Ku had started out indignant and then apologetic, but now he seemed to be saying, So what? He had almost nothing left to his name. This wasn't unusual. It was always the case for debts the company had purchased from lower-tier banks.

Debtors who'd found themselves unjustly penniless. People who had nothing left but the change in their pockets. Their stories were regrettable, but Su-ho had heard those same sob stories over and over since joining the company.

In Ku's case, he most likely had fallen on hard times and was unable to pay off his loans, resulting in a provisional seizure of his property. So off he went to a lower-tier bank to mortgage his house. Because that's what those banks were for. Ku knew he was borrowing more money, but thought, once the seizure was lifted, he would be able to sell his house and pay off his debts. He didn't think this way because he was especially stupid. Anyone in his position would have thought the same thing. And he nearly did manage to sell his house. Several times. It was old, but the lot was big—big enough to consider knocking down the single-family house and putting up a multi-unit building for rental income. This is where it goes without saying that the loan officer at the bank refused to sign off on any of the purchase agreements. They abused their authority: without the consent of the mortgagee, the mortgage could not be closed or canceled. And so Ku's debt grew, his house did not sell, and he was forced to take out yet another loan.

Just like that, it was over for him. He lost everything. The bank sold his debt to David. Most of Su-ho's cases had lost everything this way. Banks never sold a customer's debt until they'd reached the point of diminishing returns.

Su-ho knew all too well how debt happened. The debtors did not. They did not know as well as he, how being careless with money could turn into debt, and how debt could snowball, and how quickly it could bury you. All they did was act puzzled, then aggrieved, then angry, then defiant.

Sending a notice demanding repayment and taking the debtor to court when he didn't comply was pointless. All it did was legally confirm that the debt still existed. It was the same with compulsory execution. In most cases, there was nothing to salvage. And if the debtor filed for bankruptcy, everyone was left with a headache. Pushing for repayment only led to more legal fees, and the money recouped ended up being less than the principal and inter-est. You had to do whatever it took to grab whatever bit of money you could before it reached that point.

Su-ho had performed due diligence on Ki-in Ku and deter-mined that the only thing there to salvage were some measly household goods that wouldn't be of interest even to a junk shop. Ku had promised to submit payments, albeit in tiny amounts, each time his daughter brought home her paycheck from her part-time job in a restaurant, and in fact he'd kept his word for a good two months. Of course, it was only fifty or a hundred thousand won each time. Which meant that Su-ho's cut was no more than five or ten thousand won. It was barely enough to cover the cost of traveling all the way to Ansan to collect payments from Ku.

"How do you figure these people end up like this?" the team leader had asked Su-ho after his first week with the company, while handing him his first assignment.

"Uh, w-w-well . . ." Su-ho stuttered.

The team leader got impatient.

"If you say it's because they're losers, then you're the true loser."

Su-ho, who'd been on the verge of saying exactly that, clapped his mouth shut and looked dumbly at the team leader.

"Debt collectors need to know at least this much: 'I get it, it's not your fault. The world has tricked you, and I can explain how.' That's the attitude you need to have. Why? So you don't get your ass handed to you. It'll boost your confidence."

"Yes, sir."

"Ugh, you're such a yes-man. No matter what I say, it's yessir, yessir, from you."

Su-ho hung his head, and the team leader stroked it, his big hand caressing Su-ho's hair as if it belonged to a tamed animal. It usually made him angry to have someone touch his head, but when the team leader did it, Su-ho felt nearly teary-eyed with gratitude.

"Listen. This is what the experts say. The real problem is unregulated finance. It gets everyone addicted to low interest rates. They drop the rates and lend money to just about anyone. Then people can't pay it back and wind up in debt. They mistake those loans for their own money and buy themselves cars and houses. That cash is not their own, but you know what they tell themselves? No worries. Because there's something they can always trust. Real estate. Land doesn't lie, they think. So they buy apartments and they buy land. It's true. Land doesn't lie. But the market does. When the market freezes, real estate is the first to freeze with it. Stagnant consumption, weakened household finances, real estate slumps—they all go together, like gears, turning each other. Those gears turn and turn until the working class is ruined."

"Sir?"

"The government always bails out banks before families. And the bailout stops just as soon as the system is restored. They line each other's pockets and don't give a shit about the little people. They don't care if they go under or even if they die. Do you get what I'm saying? People don't end up poor because they're stupid. They end up poor because the system is fucked."

"Yes, sir."

"'Yes, sir,' what? Are you even capable of repeating any of that back to me? If not, then you still have no idea. So just remember this. Some of the more educated debtors like to get up on their high horse and go on about how it's not their fault, it's the world's fault. But remember: no one made those assholes do it. They fucked themselves over. They got greedy and borrowed money and fucked themselves. Got it? It's even in the Bible. 'The wicked borrow and do not repay, but the righteous give generously.' Would God have said that if it weren't a big deal? Those assholes who don't pay off their debts are evildoers, every single one of them."

Of course, knowing that changed nothing. The best method was to stop being greedy while you still had something worth holding on to. If you wanted to cancel your debt, you had to be willing to let go of your house. But debtors were always angling for a way to hold on to their stuff while having their debts forgiven.

Ki-in Ku was no different. He pretended not to know that clinging to his house had caused him to lose everything. He was convinced he'd been hoodwinked by a society that drives people into debt. Su-ho's plan was to remind Ku he still had something worth protecting after all. All he had to do was mention the name of the restaurant where Ku's daughter worked, and Ku would think long and hard about "what he had left." There was only one piece of advice Su-ho could offer him. To do whatever it takes while you're still alive. Because once you're dead, you can't do anything.

He rang the doorbell.

"It's me, Su-ho Lee."

There was no sound. It was as quiet as an abandoned house. That's how it usually went. In a crisis, everyone plays possum. But when threatened just a little bit, they squirm and run away like rats.

Su-ho still remembered most of what the team leader had told him, but there was one thing in particular that he remembered with perfect clarity.

"When it comes down to it, everyone deserves pity. Is it okay to hit someone and threaten them and take advantage of their weaknesses just because they're a debtor? Of course not, right? Of course not. That's not how people should treat each other. Is it okay for a human being to strike another human being? To curse at them? To take their things? Of course it's not okay. Got it? That's not how people should behave. That said . . ."

The team leader had paused there and stared at Su-ho. Su-ho swallowed. The team leader smiled. It was a very puzzling and contradictory smile. In a word, a human smile.

"It's okay to treat an *animal* that way. For us, I mean. We throw frogs against rocks to kill them. We crush bugs to death with our bare hands. We kick dogs. We even roast or boil them for food. Debtors are not people. If they were truly human, they would never be so irresponsible and incompetent. They're bugs. They're rats. They're frogs. They have to work to qualify as dogs."

Su-ho hawked up a gob of phlegm from deep inside, spit it on the ground and rubbed it in with the sole of his shoe, then loudly kicked the front gate. The animal in the house would cower at the sound. If the gate opened, Su-ho might step inside and kick the animal the same way. If it didn't open, he would climb over the wall and do it anyway, and if he climbed the wall but the animal was gone, he would do whatever it took to track it down and do the same.

He kicked the door harder. Su-ho Lee was setting a rat trap. He was spraying bug spray. This was not a human being's house he was calling at. He was knocking on the door of a doghouse.

12

When does evil intent become evil itself? Is it evil simply to imagine and harbor an idea? Does it begin when a thought is put into action? And if that action fails, then did evil never exist to begin with?

If indeed there was no evil, then is it okay to allow bad intentions to make you change your behavior, move to a new place, transform your life? Does that mean evil thoughts are no worse than a daydream, a mere fantasy? Even fantasies and daydreams can sometimes alter reality.

In Se-oh's case, when did she first harbor ill will? Was it when she heard that man's name from Detective Kim? Was it when she saw her father wrapped in bandages, or when she never got to show him how she looked in the purple coat he'd bought for her? Perhaps it began the day after she'd spent those nights alone in the charred hull of #157. Or maybe it started much later than that, such as the moment she set her chopsticks down, unable to finish eating the ramen that refused to taste the same as the ramen her father had made for her, no matter that it was the same stuff. Or during one of the many random echoes of her father's nagging that would ring suddenly in her ears.

Maybe it began the moment she first laid eyes on the neither large nor menacing-looking Su-ho. Or the moment he looked to her less like someone who would drive another person to kill themselves and more like the kind of coward who would go into hysterics upon witnessing a death. Maybe it was the moment she saw his filthy habit of spitting on the ground all the time, just as she'd imagined he would. Or when she realized it was unfair to blame everything on him. Or, maybe it began after she'd felt the unfamiliar thrill that comes only when you amplify your malice.

Truth is, all of it was the starting point. Those scattered moments had somehow converged, each point forming a line that surrounded Se-oh to reach this current moment.

For Se-oh, evil intent was like a weapon that was simultaneously hot yet cold, hard yet soft, sharp yet blunt, heavy yet light. Her heart would boil as hot as a blast furnace then cool to ice, a rapidly increasing cycle spurred on by the core of that malice.

Se-oh's bad intention was the hammer she'd found in #157. If she were to put it to use, it would be for its blunt force. She hadn't known at first what she might use it for, but the hammer had found its own use. To keep herself from immediately wielding it, she sometimes had to convince herself that the time was not quite right, but the opportunity *was* coming, and wouldn't be long now.

If she were to swing that hammer, there was no question she would aim for the brain. It was the perfect target for a single strike. As organs go, the brain had such a high rate of fatality. It was much more likely to result in immediate death than a blow to the heart.

Of course, she could aim elsewhere. Like the back or chest, whose larger surface areas offered a higher probability of not missing, or the arms or legs, which she could still easily hit while swinging wildly. Even if all she did was put him in a hospital bed for a month, that would be enough. Assuming, of course, that she'd be content with only breaking a few veins or capillaries. Certainly not if her intention was to kill.

The brain's surface area is equal to about a single sheet of newspaper and takes up no more than 2 percent of the average adult's body weight, or about 3.3 pounds. That small organ can control a person who stands over five and a half feet tall. It tells them to eat, to take the bus, to hold a grudge, to hate, and to make decisions both monumental and trivial that change their lives. It cheats and lies and placates and clings. It threatens and blackmails and violates and commands. It fills a man's mind with thoughts of death and compels him to take his own life.

Carbon monoxide, or even just too much cigarette smoke, attacks the brain first, damaging the tissue by depriving it of oxygen. The brain is particularly vulnerable to heat. As Se-oh struggled to imagine the agony of a brain, a body, a home, a world being wrapped in flames, she tightened her grip on the hammer.

Her task was clear. To bring the hammer down hard on something.

Ssshhh.

The air made a vicious sound as the hammer punched through it. The sound alone had enough force to rattle a brain.

A few more practice swings, and Se-oh knew that raising her arm overhead and bringing it down fast and hard generated the most force. But to aim for *his* brain, she would have to be taller than Su-ho. She wasn't, which meant a single blow wouldn't be fatal. He would fight back hard against this unexplained attack. She would have to swing the hammer and run like hell, or else find herself caught.

After watching Su-ho come out of the debtor's house and spit on the ground again, Se-oh turned to head for the subway station. Soon, she heard him behind her; then he was overtaking her, his pace much faster than hers.

She lost him in the crowd of commuters heading home. She'd grown careless, having been to the same location several times before. But she had her guesses as to where he'd go next. The row of restaurants along the main road. He was a regular there.

She checked one after the other. No sign of him. Keeping up with him was one thing, but guessing when he was hungry or what he wanted to eat was another thing entirely. She headed back toward the station and spotted him. He was sitting in a noodle shop, staring blankly at the television mounted to the wall, waiting for his food. It was the first time he'd gone to that particular restaurant.

Finding him this time had had nothing to do with the statistics or probabilities that she'd calculated from her painstaking observations. It was simply dumb luck. Realizing that made her want to end it now. Why drag it out any longer, when she could just bash him over the head with the hammer she kept in her bag as he was exiting the restaurant? It would happen so fast, he'd be unable to defend himself. It wasn't unusual to be attacked by a complete stranger in a crowded place.

But she couldn't. This task, it was akin to an inevitability, or a duty. She had to curb her impulses until the time was right. A mere impulse could not possibly contain all of the fury and hatred that she felt. She would find a better method than the hammer. And she would gladly keep company with malice until she did.

Malice gave Se-oh something to do. It swept away her grief and lifted her out of bed in the morning. It gave her energy and got her moving. It fed her and kept her going from place to place instead of lying in bed all day. It enabled her to live simply, and without complaints, in the cramped goshiwon room barely big enough to hold a twin bed and a small desk. It helped her endure the hot nights in that windowless room where she would lay still so as not to make a sound. It got her through the hours spent never talking to another soul. And it kept her from returning to the ashes of #157.

Se-oh left Su-ho at the restaurant and walked slowly back to the station. There was only one entrance. If she hid among the crowd, she could wait for him unseen and ride back on the subway with him. She was not alone. No matter the time or place, Su-ho was with her.

Sometimes she thought about attacking Su-ho so much that she wondered if it hadn't already happened. She had trouble distinguishing between it and things that had actually taken place. It was the future, and yet it felt like the past. The way she saw it in her mind was so concrete and clear and detailed that she questioned whether she was truly picturing something that hadn't happened or was in fact recalling something that had, even though all she had to go on was speculation and wild leaps rather than known facts or self-evident cause and effect. The very lack of logic or validation had dug in deep. Se-oh was way past being able to tell the difference.

13

Contrary to its name, Sunshine Goshiwon was buried at the farthest end of the alley where no sunlight could reach. It being summer, the shade would probably keep the inside cool, but come winter, it would be unbearably frigid. The building was so old that the paint was flaking off in great, flapping strips, as if someone had plastered the walls with flyers. The foundation stone was so worn down that the date of construction was no longer legible. The windows in the landing were all smashed out; on stormy days, the stairs and corridors would flood. Taped over the name of the grilled tripe restaurant on the ground floor was a FOR LEASE sign. The windows on the second and third floors were blocked out with black paper. The goshiwon was on the fourth floor.

Ki-jeong dialed the phone number posted at the first-floor entrance.

"Sunshine."

"Is this the goshiwon?"

"Yes, this is Sunshine."

"I'd like to check out a room."

"One hundred or one hundred thirty at three hundred."

"Excuse me?"

"The deposit's three hundred thousand won. Rent is one hundred thousand for no window, or one hundred thirty thousand for a window."

"Oh, wow."

"It's the cheapest you'll find around here. As you probably know, for a place like this—"

"It's not that. I was surprised at *how* cheap it is."

"Too cheap for you? Then take the one thirty room. The cheaper one *is* a bit much, even for me. It's best to just think of it as a patch of ground and a roof over your head. When do you need to move in?"

"Well, I'd like to see the room in person first."

"Goshiwon are all the same. I'm sure it's no different from the last place you saw. And anyway, I don't have an empty room for you to look at."

"Excuse me?"

"You're third on the waiting list. A room will open up in about two months. Maybe sooner. Nowadays everyone comes and goes so quickly, you never can tell. So, joining us? What's your name?"

Ki-jeong hung up. She wasn't shocked that such a cheap place existed. It was the way the woman had asked, "Joining us?" The tone of the woman's voice scared her. It seemed to say that once Ki-jeong was in she would never get back out again.

Ki-jeong hadn't sought this quest; the quest had come to her. She couldn't even be sure whether it was for her sister's sake at all. It might be, and it might not be. How could Ki-jeong assume that her sister would want her poking around, asking questions, looking for the person her sister had been trying to contact? She'd started it in order to shake off the guilt of knowing her sister had died alone, to escape the thoughts that tormented her. And she'd wanted to distance herself from anything that reminded her of her current situation, whatever it took. She wanted to distance herself from Do-jun's rage. Nothing filled that empty space better than her sister.

It was hard to wrap her brain around Do-jun. He kept sending her text messages filled with profanities. After a while, every time she got a pornographic spam text with a dirty photo attached, or a text advertising low-interest loans, or sales ads for shopping sites she'd never registered for, or text messages with phone numbers for designated-driver-for-hire services that came at all hours, day and night, she obsessed over the idea that Do-jun had somehow sent them to her.

Every time she left her apartment building, Do-jun was there, glaring at her from a distance, before walking away. Even when he should have been in class, there he was. He left rocks and crushed soda cans in her mailbox. He banged on her apartment door in the middle of the night and shouted outside her window, waking her.

If she'd stopped for a second to ask herself how Do-jun could possibly have sent so many different spam texts, or figured out the code to get into her apartment building and access her mailbox, or loiter in front of her building in the middle of a school day, she would've realized that her suspicions were full of holes. But she did not ask. Everything bad that happened to her, she pinned on Do-jun.

She got angry at first. It was all so melodramatic—Do-jun's resentment, his victim mentality, and the hatred and anger that came from it. He couldn't imagine that *he* would ever be treated unfairly. Such a typical spoiled child, overprotected, never met a single obstacle in his life.

After a while, she took a hard look at herself. She'd gotten a lot of things wrong. Using grades as a way to keep kids in line, skimming their essays because the content was invariably predictable and boring, scoring their work based on their attitudes or personalities, and thus grading them according to her own assumptions or prejudices rather than their individual efforts or achievements, never failing to scold or sound sarcastic when she spoke to them, letting their stories and explanations go in one ear and out the other, being stingy with praise and questioning their intentions, not bothering to conceal from them how exhausted the work made her.

Ki-jeong had been put through enough. She was the one who'd ended up punished, not him. Her punishment had been socially sanctioned, unlike the lashing she'd given him. But if she hadn't taken the matter into her own hands, as it were, she would have had no other recourse. Just like that, Do-jun was made the victim and got off scot-free.

Was hitting a student a couple of times—for educational purposes, of course—really so much worse than intentionally getting a teacher in trouble? Maybe in some cases it was. Ki-jeong knew the real problem was the malice behind her actions. It was whenever she managed to quiet her frustration that she recalled the thrill she'd felt while hitting Do-jun. She understood that was why she had to be disciplined. Bad thoughts were pungent, like garlic or ginger. Once the smell was on you, you couldn't hide it.

If she apologized sincerely, would she be forgiven? But how could she be sincere when she didn't know what she'd done wrong?

Would she feel better once the child's anger had subsided? Would she feel like her life was starting over fresh?

Even if she tried to apologize, Do-jun would just ignore her. She'd bumped into him a while back and loudly called out his name. He'd glanced over his shoulder but kept going. She had run after him in desperation. Not to get angry at him, she told herself, though her urgent pursuit had every semblance of anger. If she couldn't close the distance between them, she would never get the chance to talk to him.

After Do-jun had run so far from her that she couldn't catch him, she breathed freely again. It was a good thing she couldn't speak to him. She felt relieved not to give him the impression that everything was resolved. It was only fair for him to live in a world of resentment, where he blamed everyone else, and where someone hated him. No one else had done that to him. He'd brought it on himself.

But she couldn't really convince herself of that. The opportunity for reconciliation had been lost. She didn't know whether it was she or Do-jun who'd misplaced it. She just wanted to run from everything. But she couldn't move away or change her phone number, or else she'd have to tell her mother what had happened, and she wasn't ready to do that. Once her mother found out, there would be no consoling her. The idea of her daughter, her sole pride and joy, possibly never recovering from the blow to her career would fill her with despair, and she would genuinely dread that outcome. She might even say to Ki-jeong, "You'll turn out just like *her*." Ki-jeong, too, feared that she would fail and her life would amount to nothing, "just like her."

Ki-jeong had been in middle school the first time she met her newborn baby sister. Their meeting took place at the mistress's house. The thought of her mother at home alone kept Ki-jeong from being affectionate. Instead, she channeled her mother's hatred and contempt for the infant. She could sense how much pain her half-sister was causing her mother. Her father looked happy. The baby kept on smiling and innocently sucking on its fingers and sometimes its toes, babbling something unintelligible. It was adorable. The baby gave her a vague understanding of how life was made up of ambivalent things.

Ki-jeong never wanted her parents to be angry at her, so she always asked first what they wanted from her. She reduced conflict by putting their expectations before her own desires. Sometimes she asked simply because she didn't know what she wanted.

Her sister's life had seemed preferable to hers in some ways. From early on, her sister had had a knack for disregarding whatever she didn't want to deal with. She never tried to win Ki-jeong's mother's love, nor did she seem particularly troubled by its absence. Ki-jeong suffered constantly from her own neediness for her mother's affection, despite the unremitting love and care she received from her, but her sister suffered no such luxury.

Ki-jeong was forever anxious and worried, despite her highly conscientious and organized lifestyle; meanwhile, her younger sister had always been quiet yet brave, relaxed despite having nothing, able to fly by the seat of her pants in the face of an uncertain future. What made her sister that way? What would drive a sister like that to kill herself? And would this Se-oh Yun person be able to provide answers to these belated questions?

Ki-jeong had gotten hopelessly lost while searching for #157. The alleyways all looked so similar, and none of the houses displayed their street addresses. As she made yet another round of the neighborhood, Ki-jeong suppressed the desire to give up and go home. She told herself this visit would bring an end to her search. The problem being, she didn't know what she was hoping to find.

After dropping in to a real estate office to double-check the location, she finally found it, and understood at once why the real estate agent had looked so guarded when she'd asked about #157. Ki-jeong went back to the office to ask what had happened, but the agent wouldn't tell her. That was strange. Weren't people usually eager to gossip about misfortune? Perhaps whatever had happened at #157 was too serious to allow for that kind of frivolity.

She was at a loss. All she had accomplished was verifying that she'd once again failed to find Se-oh Yun. She slowly made her way back through the maze of alleys. She'd thought she was nearing the end of her search, but it hadn't even started yet. How was she to begin?

The police officer in charge of her sister's case scolded her, saying he'd warned her there was no point in searching. Ki-jeong stared back undaunted. As if he had personally spirited Se-oh Yun away from #157. He grimaced with impatience and muttered about how busy he was.

There was one place she thought of that could help find people when the police wouldn't. She hesitated over whether to make the call, but the process turned out to be simpler than she'd thought. She didn't even have to go in person. She simply explained the situation over the phone and wired a deposit.

"No problem," the employee said. "We'll get on this right away."

Of course, it didn't go quite as promised. The employee called back to say it was a tougher case than they'd thought. There were no cell phone accounts or credit card bills or Internet search histories to be found.

Ki-jeong assumed this part was a formality. The harder the search, the higher the fee, after all. They wouldn't be satisfied unless they could claim that even the easiest of jobs was difficult. Being new to this, Ki-jeong was very nervous about getting cheated. But she'd already paid the deposit, and so each time the employee mentioned an additional fee, she hesitated a little and then logged on to her online bank account again.

It took three months for the employee's voice to turn triumphant.

"We got a hit."

They explained that Se-oh's name had appeared on a job search website. She had responded to a grocery store's help wanted ad and submitted a resume. The resume had the phone number for Sunshine Goshiwon.

Had Se-oh gone to school with her sister? How close were they? Se-oh Yun, formerly of #157. Se-oh Yun, aspiring grocery store worker. Se-oh Yun, resident of Sunshine Goshiwon. Se-oh Yun, who didn't even have her own cell phone and had to use the goshiwon's number instead. Ki-jeong's heart raced as if it were her sister who'd surfaced on that job search website.

The hallway inside the goshiwon was lined so closely with doors, they were practically touching. Each door had to be a separate room, but Ki-jeong could not believe how little space there was between them. Less than a meter wide, the hallway stretched deep into the building and was dark despite it being midday. There was a relentless smell; whatever mishap had befallen the residents of #157, something similar had happened to the residents here. It smelled like disaster. The thought of those tiny rooms packed so tightly together was shocking. It was clear, though, that the real disaster waited behind the doors.

Ki-jeong knocked at #433. The sound echoed down the hall-way. As silent as the room was, she was surrounded by noise. Televisions playing, radios blaring, water dripping, voices mur-muring, someone humming, refrigerators running, fan blades spinning, water boiling, objects falling, chairs scraping, someone hiccupping. The noise came at her from everywhere. She couldn't tell if any of it was coming from inside #433 or from the other rooms.

A door opened. It wasn't #433 but the room to the right. A disheveled shadow slipped out. It looked at first like a puff of dark smoke, and then like something gelatinous, phlegmy. The object dragged its phlegmy feet and vanished into the darkness at the end of the hallway. Ki-jeong was alone again. She gave the door-knob to #433 a try, then headed back down the airless, stuffy hallway and out of the goshiwon.

14

At Ki-jeong's mother's house, the door to her sister's room was always closed. It was closed when she vanished without a word a few years earlier, and when she came back. It was closed when she left home again, and when Ki-jeong held a simple funeral for her, alone. Ki-jeong had never once found the closed door strange. It seemed natural, as if it were a door to a utility room or a storage closet.

Ki-jeong didn't even think to enter the room until after returning from Sunshine Goshiwon. The room was relatively pristine. Without anyone to occupy it, it felt chilly despite the summer heat, but it wasn't the kind of chill you felt in an actual storage closet or a basement. It was more akin to a well-sanitized and organized hospital.

She poked around a little, but other than guessing from the layers of dust just how much time had passed, she didn't think she'd learn much from it. It looked like its previous occupant had purposefully cleaned it out before leaving.

She didn't skip over the locked drawer, though. She got a screwdriver from the toolbox and managed to pry it open after a few tries. She made so much noise doing so that her mother came running. Her mother stopped right before the threshold, as if something bad might happen if she crossed it, and clucked her tongue at Ki-jeong.

"That's what all that racket was? What on earth are you looking for? And where is that girl, anyway? School's out for the summer, but she doesn't so much as call or show up? That's disrespectful, even for her."

Ki-jeong didn't respond. She wanted to delay telling her mother about her sister's death for as long as possible. Delaying it wouldn't change the fact of her death, after all. She was pretty sure she would be hurt by her mother's reaction. Her sister, already being dead, of course, wouldn't be hurt no matter what Ki-jeong's mother said or did.

There were no diaries or appointment books. The desk calendar was blank; she hadn't marked so much as her own birthday on it. The locked drawer revealed two notebooks, neither of which had been used. Ki-jeong leafed through her sister's books, but nothing was underlined.

She read the titles of the books out loud, hoping one of them might offer a hint. *Aesthetic Theory. Blood and Champagne: The Life and Times of Robert Capa. Aroma: The Cultural History of Smell. The God of Small Things. Dog of the Underworld. First Love. The Silent Cry.* The only thing those titles revealed was that her sister was interested in a lot of different things but didn't delve deeply into any of them. She had left not a single clue behind that revealed anything of herself.

Ki-jeong had always considered her sister careless, sloppy, and incapable of expressing her own opinion, and thought she'd masked the low self-esteem that came from growing up in someone else's house with a smile that projected innocence and confidence. It was possible, though, that her sister had chosen to conceal herself in order to live in harmony with the new family that she'd suddenly found herself a part of. In fact, maybe she was far more in control than Ki-jeong had thought, to the point where she'd foreseen what would happen and had meticulously erased all traces of herself well in advance.

On one of her rounds, Ki-jeong visited her sister's old high school. Her homeroom teacher still remembered her. On the spur of the moment, Ki-jeong lied and said her sister was missing. She figured she might get further that way. Her sister's teacher was shocked to hear it and helped her to find contact information for several of her sister's old friends.

Of the people Ki-jeong contacted, only one was willing to meet her. Another had simply changed her number and was unreachable, and a third reacted coldly at the mention of her sister's name and claimed she hadn't known her all that well. From the way they spoke to Ki-jeong, she could tell they didn't hold her sister in high regard and weren't exactly itching for an update. They all seemed put off by being contacted out of the blue. Ki-jeong understood. There could be nothing inviting about getting a phone call from a family member of a friend you hadn't spoken to in ages.

The one girl who agreed to meet Ki-jeong told her she had just graduated from college and was preparing for the civil service exam. Most people her age were doing something like that. It was the age at which you were in a constant state of preparing for something, or failing at what you'd prepared to do only to try again. The age at which you tried endlessly to fulfill something but had no fulfillment to call your own.

The girl, who'd been in the same class as her sister, told her they were only passing acquaintances and that they had not talked after graduation. Ki-jeong prodded a bit more, but the girl seemed unaware of her sister's family life or the issues surrounding it. She couldn't recall anything specific, like her sister's habits or which celebrities she'd liked. No matter what Ki-jeong asked, the girl said, "You know, she was just quiet and smiled a lot . . ." Toward the end, she apologized for wasting Ki-jeong's time when she clearly did not know her sister well at all.

When Ki-jeong asked if the girl could at least steer her toward someone who might know something, the girl hesitated and said, "Actually, there were rumors."

"What rumors?"

"People complaining about how she tricked them. They said she would call and offer to hook them up with a part-time job, but when they met her in person, it turned out to be a multi-level marketing scam."

"Multi-level marketing?"

"Yeah, everyone was talking about it. Even I heard about it, and I barely knew her. It was all over the news at the time, too. All this stuff about illegal pyramid schemes . . . What I heard was that they were treating college kids like slaves, feeding everyone scraps and making guys and girls who didn't even know each other all sleep in the same room. Those stories had everyone so scared that whenever you got a call from someone you hadn't heard from in a while, you automatically assumed they were trying to lure you into one. Then, one day, I really did get a call from her. I mean, we'd never once spoken on the phone before. . . . We really weren't that close. I could barely put a face to her name. It was the same for everyone else I knew, too. They said she was going through the yearbook and cold-calling everyone. I'd heard so many stories at that point that the moment she said her name I just hung up. I'm sorry about that."

"I don't blame you."

"I was afraid that once she started talking, I would fall for whatever she said. They say those people really have a way with words. You can't listen to them for even a second or they'll have you. She kept trying to call for a while after that, but I never answered. And then finally the calls stopped."

Was that it? Her sister's tightly guarded secret? The moment Ki-jeong heard the words *multi-level marketing scam*, she could see how all the pieces of the puzzle fit together. The debt the detective had mentioned made more sense now, too. Her sister had bet everything she had, hoping it would pay off, only to fail, and when she couldn't get out from under her debts, she'd offered up her life instead.

From there, Ki-jeong was able to contact others who'd known her sister and finally meet some who'd been with her in the pyramid scheme's so-called dorm. This time she told them right away that her sister was dead. It was the easiest way to explain why she was calling. Each time, they all expressed the same shock and gave her the same formulaic words of consolation.

Their stories were identical. How ardently she had tried to fool them, how big of a front she'd put up to keep them from leaving, how she kept rattling off the same words to try to seduce them over to her wild ideas. Ki-jeong wasn't sure how much to believe. But whether she believed them or not, it wasn't out of the ordinary. The fact that it was so different from the sister she'd known was no excuse. It was only natural that the sister she knew would be different from the person her sister's friends had known.

When she failed to react with sympathy, one of her sister's

friends said, sounding aggrieved, "I was trapped there for three months because of your sister. I missed an entire semester and lost all of my tuition money. My mom was so mad at me."

"The stuff my sister told you was that convincing?"

"At the time, it was."

"Then who was the one who tricked my sister into joining?"

"You mean her upline?"

"Upline?"

"The one who recruited her. Wow, I can't believe I still remember those terms. They really drilled it into us. Those are the terms they used. Upline for recruiters, downline for recruits."

"So when you recruit a friend, they become your downline?"

"Yes, I was her downline."

"Who was her upline?"

Ki-jeong's voice trembled slightly. Maybe she'd finally found a link between Se-oh Yun and her sister.

"Some guy named Bu-wi."

"Bu-wi?"

"He graduated high school before us. He was her boyfriend."

Everything about her sister was new to Ki-jeong. Including the fact that she'd had a boyfriend.

"What about Se-oh Yun? Was there someone by that name there?"

"Who's that?"

"You don't know her?"

"Did she die with her?"

The girl looked apologetic as soon as the words were out. But there was nothing to be sorry for. It was normal for someone her age to be a little rude and insensitive when it came to death.

After returning home, Ki-jeong looked up a book on network

marketing. According to the book, one could drastically reduce the number of years spent toiling simply by making a slight alteration to how one toiled. It said to utilize personal networks as a shortcut. Consumers could become salespeople, without the retail or wholesale middleman, and expand their markets through a chain of personal connections. As their downline increased exponentially, they could earn the equivalent of an ordinary officer worker's thirty-nine-year salary in just one year.

The book didn't explain where that thirty-nine-year figure had come from. Instead it kept repeating how the profit model worked. How you could increase your downline from one to two recruits, and then ten, and so on, and how those on the downline would command their own downline, earning you a massive, unbelievable profit ratio.

The core idea was that by investing a year's work, you could rest easy for the next thirty-nine. That is, by enduring hardship for just one year, you were guaranteed to succeed, and so you had to view a few months of suffering as a kind of investment capital. It was only by clinging tenaciously to survival that you would accomplish whatever you set out to do. Giving up meant certain failure, but holding out for a year raised your chances for success.

Did people really fall for something so obvious? That not everyone would achieve success, but everyone would for sure work like a dog, and that, in the end, only a very few would be spared from total failure? Did they really buy the exaggerated description of ideal circumstances and the repeated tripe about how if you just worked hard enough, you could strike it rich? Ki-jeong was dubious, and yet considering how many people fell for it, there was clearly a convincing angle to it.

Ki-jeong kept going. She went back to the school to look for

Bu-wi. It was relatively easy for her to do, since she'd been a teacher.

But while the process was easy, finding Bu-wi turned out to be another story. His phone number was out of service, someone else was living at his address, and the college that he'd claimed he was attending informed her that no one by that name had ever enrolled or graduated from there.

Ki-jeong repeated the name Bu-wi out loud. She wrote her sister's name on a piece of paper, wrote Bu-wi next to it, and drew a circle around each name. She drew a line between the circles to connect them. She made an upline and a downline. Then she wrote the name Se-oh and tried connecting all three circles as many ways as she could. First, her sister, then Se-oh, then Bu-wi. She could change the order as much as she wanted. No matter how she drew the line—from Se-oh to her sister to Bu-wi, or her sister to Bu-wi to Se-oh—they were always connected. Everything was possible in her imagination, because she really didn't know any of them. She stared hard at the lines that stretched off in all directions while simultaneously remaining in place. As if the owners of those lines were right there. As if by staring at their names, she was seeing their faces.

Back when their lives had connected, they'd probably had no idea that, in just a few years' time, one of them would meet a lonely death. And that no one would mourn her.

15

Wu-sul Kim had been far too stubborn about hiring. He'd rejected out of hand nearly every job application that he'd received via the job search website. A few had appealed to him. A very small handful of applicants had struck him as outgoing and earnest. But they in turn had taken one look at his grocery store and lost all interest. They didn't bother to hide their disappointment when they learned that their future place of employment was little more than a hole-in-the-wall grocery tucked inside a drab commercial arcade in an apartment complex. When he interviewed them, they responded to his questions with an obvious lack of interest, or fired back by asking how much his annual sales were.

After that, he realized he'd be better off hiring someone who applied in person rather than online. In large letters, he wrote NOW HIRING: HELP SERVICE PLANNER on poster board and hung it in the front window. Jae-hyung Shin smirked and called the job title pretentious. Wu-sul wasn't crazy about it either, but he refused to change it. He liked the vagueness of it. His plan was to hire the first person who asked him what it meant. But no one asked, let alone submitted an application.

"That's because you made it *too* vague. Employee, staff, assistant, worker—that's what you usually see on a job ad. But 'help service planner'? And in English, no less. What does that even mean?"

Jae-hyung, the grocery's sole employee, wouldn't stop nagging Wu-sul about the need to hire someone new. From the way he told it, the long days and heavy workload had him at the brink of death.

"I wrote it that way on purpose," Wu-sul said. "Whoever gets the job needs to be at least smart enough to get what I mean right away. And if not, then they should be confident and not feel embarrassed to ask. What's so hard about asking, 'What's that? What does it mean?'"

"Okay, but what's so hard about writing it the normal way instead? 'Now hiring part-time.' Clear and simple."

"Absolutely not. This is a permanent full-time position."

"You can't be serious! That might not be what any of the applicants are looking for. Who would want to work in a place like this permanently?"

"You have no clue because you grew up sheltered. You don't appreciate the woes of the disposable worker."

"Sure, sure. I've also never been forced into an early retirement like you were."

"Keep talking to your boss that way, and maybe you will be."

"Don't listen to me. Hire whoever you want! If you want a part-timer, hire a part-timer. You want someone full time, then hire them full time."

"I will. And I'll interview every applicant, no matter what's on their resume."

He'd said that last part jokingly, but when Se-oh offered him her application, Wu-sul couldn't help stealing a glance over at Jae-hyung. Jae-hyung looked exhausted from rushing to one address after another, trying to keep up with the onslaught of afternoon deliveries. Wu-sul knew that when he said he was dying, he wasn't entirely exaggerating.

Jae-hyung gave him a look that said, Hurry up and take it. Wu-sul pretended not to understand and looked back and forth between Se-oh and the white envelope she was holding out, as if he didn't know what it was. Se-oh kept her eyes fixed on the floor. She did not bow and say, I would like to apply for the position, or add any unnecessary niceties like, I hope that you will consider my application, or smile politely so as to leave a positive impression. She acted like she didn't know what it was she held in her hand either. Nor did she look like she was debating how she should react.

Wu-sul had no choice but to finally ask, "Is that a job application?"

Se-oh gave the faintest of nods. Her head barely moved. She was not a small woman. Wu-sul's wife was a big woman, but Se-oh dwarfed her. Whenever his wife moved even the tiniest bit, her large shadow swayed every which way, but Se-oh didn't seem to move at all. She was a stationary object. Even her shadow appeared nailed in place. She didn't actually nod her head so much as give an impression of having nodded. No part of her moved, except maybe for a slight fluttering of her eyelids.

"We're looking for a help service planner. Do you know what that entails?"

Wu-sul asked because he wanted to hear what her voice sounded like.

"Is it not a sales position?" Se-oh asked languidly.

To his surprise, he liked her answer. He'd had a few answers in

mind that would have been an automatic no. Specifically, anything that contained phrases like "happy customers" or "customer
satisfaction." He loathed answers that overpackaged basic business transactions. Grocery stores sold products, not customer service. There was no point in exhausting yourself emotionally with
all that kindness this and friendliness that. He didn't object to
friendly service, of course, but running a grocery store came down
to selling good products. He also wasn't crazy about job applicants
who tried too hard to dress up sales with big, multisyllabic words
like capital, business, enterprise, marketing, and so on. He was
tired of assigning useless meanings to things. It was fine to simply
say that grocery stores were places where products were bought
and sold.

That said, he was damned if he was going to hire Se-oh. As
much as he downplayed the idea of friendly customer service,
there was no way he could hire that gruff, shadow-like, mountain
of a woman. As she said, it was a sales position, but sales meant
exchanging goods for cash, and, in a grocery store, the one handing you their cash was, after all, a human being.

"We're only hiring men."

For some reason, he had to summon his courage to lie to her.
The crushed silhouette of her oversized shadow seemed to give
off an equally large presence. Wu-sul was struck by it, and he
couldn't stop staring. Se-oh didn't seem particularly disappointed
as she slowly put the envelope back in the pocket of her purple
trench coat, which made no sense for the weather, and left the
grocery store.

Jae-hyung stared accusingly at Wu-sul. Wu-sul tried to avoid
his gaze but then gave up and ran out of the shop, calling to Se-oh
as she headed toward the park. He called out twice quietly, then

once loudly. Se-oh turned, her face devoid of any giddy hope or expectation that she might actually have a shot at getting the job. Nor did the flatness of her expression seem to have anything to do with the potential job being at a mere grocery store. It looked like it was the only expression she could make.

Wu-sul sat across from her in the cramped storage room where he conducted all of his job interviews and slowly examined her application. As he'd suspected, there wasn't much to it. After dropping out of college, she hadn't worked anywhere at all. At least five years appeared unaccounted for. What had she been doing during that time? Even as the question occurred to him, Wu-sul marveled at himself for wondering. *Who cares?* he thought. At the same time, he knew why he wondered. It was because she didn't seem desperate or ready to beg for a job. Nor was it because she was calculating in some other way. It was simply how she carried herself. She seemed to have no attachments. That thought answered another question. The question of why he was about to hire her.

Wu-sul hesitated, and then held out his hand. Se-oh stared at him blankly. He wondered for a moment if he'd made a mistake, but he didn't take back the decision. He had a good enough reason. Se-oh had appeared right when he could no longer afford not to hire someone.

"Help Service" was a meal prep delivery service. Customers called to order ready-to-cook meals, and they selected and prepped the appropriate ingredients, added the right seasonings, and delivered it to their doors. The apartment complex where the store was located held mostly smaller units with a high ratio of young, working couples. Jae-hyung was the one who'd suggested they start the service—essentially to grocery shop for their customers.

They'd flyered the complex and posted ads in local papers. As word spread that they prepped ingredients for you at a reasonable price, their customer base grew and they gained a good number of regulars. Most of the working couples they got ordered the evening meal prep service. They also took lots of orders for baby food prep and party food prep.

Se-oh was put to work at the cash register. In the afternoons, they sometimes asked for her help putting together the delivery orders as well. Her job was to prep the items and pack them in cardboard boxes organized by delivery area and time.

Orders for prepackaged food were easy: all she had to do was ask which brands they preferred and box them up. Naturally, she had to take care to check the expiration dates and the condition of the packaging. If the food was too close to expiring or if the box was dented or crushed, customers assumed the store was dumping their old inventory on them. Orders for vegetables, meat, or fish were tricky. The items had to be fresh, of course, but choosing the right size or amount was always difficult. If she wasn't careful to ask plenty of questions, the customers were sure to pick a quarrel.

For the meal prep service, Se-oh took photos while prepping the ingredients and texted them to customers. In the delivery boxes she added notes that further detailed what she had done with the items. She never called attention to the care she put into her work, though. If Wu-sul hadn't happened to open one of the boxes before it was delivered, he would never have known.

She kept the same wooden look on her face all the time, a look that wasn't well suited to someone in a service position, but she wasn't unfriendly either. She never chimed in when Jae-hyung and Wu-sul were having one of their pointless bantering sessions, but she listened. And there were many times where she said nothing all day except for greeting them when she clocked in and out. Wu-sul sometimes wished he could make her crack a smile. She seemed to yearn for the life in that supermarket even while acting indifferent to it, as if everything were meaningless to her. He marveled at how both impressions seemed to be true.

16

As demolition notices went up all throughout the area scheduled for redevelopment, including the old tenement flats near the store, the number of empty homes increased. The park had grown quieter in the early morning, and there were noticeably fewer elderly people lining up to do aerobics.

According to Wu-sul, it had started with a few old men and women scattered around the park, warming up with some light calisthenics. Then they were joined by a former aerobics instructor, and their numbers grew to the size of a flash mob. But as redevelopment began pushing residents out one after the other, they'd shrunk back down to a small group.

Though there weren't as many of them now, it made Se-oh happy to watch the rows of elderly folk moving around wildly to loud music. It reminded her of how her father used to hoist dumbbells and bark out commands, though all he'd really exercised was his mouth.

After the aerobics squad was done, a badminton club took over the park. The members warmed up by swinging their rackets around at nothing and bending forward and backward to stretch their lower backs. As the shuttlecocks took to the air, Se-oh divided her attention between their steady back-and-forth flight and the tenement flats nearby.

Commuters rushed past the park on their way to the subway. Su-ho Lee was among them. By the time the first round of badminton ended, Se-oh spotted Su-ho coming out the front door of his flat. The back of his hair was still damp, and he shook it dry with his hand as he hurried toward the station. Se-oh stood to follow him.

Seeing him renewed Se-oh's strength. But when she got within a meter of Su-ho, her heart froze, and she felt like someone was binding her limbs tight. There was no reason for him to notice her, but she made every effort to blend in anyway. Sometimes she was so self-conscious that she couldn't take her eyes off of him. Other times, she didn't dare look his way at all.

In the meantime, she had been keeping detailed notes on his daily schedule, what time he got to work and what time he got home, the people he met, his radius of activity. She'd used his mail to figure out his home phone number, his birthdate, and other information, and inferred his family relationships from it as well. She'd learned through observation what foods he preferred, what his habits were. She even knew which debtors he was pursuing and how much they owed. She'd thought that information would help her predict his actions.

But it didn't. She could never tell how he was doing or what he was feeling. He kept going to restaurants she wouldn't have guessed he would like. He didn't touch a single bowl of red bean noodles all month, only to eat a bowl every day for a week. He would take the subway every day, only to abruptly switch to the bus. It was the same when he went home. He usually exited the subway station and walked along the busy commercial street, but now and then he would make his way through the apartment construction site instead. Some days after work he would drink his fill of booze with coworkers; other days, he didn't touch a drop. Some days he cursed and swore at debtors; others, he coaxed them gently. Some days he kicked with abandon at their front doors; others, he rang the bell like a guest and waited calmly.

The one thing that never changed was his habit of spitting and rubbing the saliva into the ground with his shoe and then smoking a cigarette each and every time he came outside. He wasn't a chain-smoker, but he smoked every time he was in a new location, as if to buy himself time to get familiar with the place.

When it came to Su-ho, neither a perfect set of statistics nor absolute certainties were possible. It took Se-oh a while to get this through her head. It made no sense for her to spend the whole day tracking him and not doing any work of her own. She was better off earning at least a little bit of money and making some sort of livelihood. And financially, she had no choice.

Her lack of funds meant she increasingly found herself unable to keep up with Su-ho. There were days she had only enough for bus fare. She would lose track of him while she waited, then go off in hot pursuit only to lose him once more. Whenever he took a cab, she lost him completely. The hunger gnawing at her stomach made her more tenacious in her pursuit. Malice so easily conspired with poverty and so willingly got into bed with it. Se-oh looked on powerlessly.

Her criteria for finding a job had been simple. It had to pay enough to keep her alive, and it had to be close to where Su-ho lived. She'd found the help wanted ad a few months earlier on a job search website. After she'd narrowed her search to the right area and to jobs she actually had a shot at, the grocery store had come up. She'd filled out an application, using the goshiwon's phone number since she didn't have a cell phone, but she never got called for an interview. That didn't surprise her. Her resume might as well have been blank. Her best remaining option had been to apply for a part-time job at a convenience store nearby.

There were three convenience stores between the subway stop and the tenement flats. None of them were hiring, but she'd filled out job applications at each place anyway. The turnover at those places was likely to be high. After a couple of months, she got a call. She went for an interview and, on her way home, she happened to walk past the grocery store. To her surprise, there was a job ad posted right in the window.

She was even more surprised and happy to find herself hired. It'd been a long time since she felt that way. Knowing that Su-ho lived nearby was what made her happy. To Se-oh, malice was not a fleeting emotion that stirred temporary ripples as it passed. She confirmed this every time she accompanied Su-ho on his morning commute. Malice never grew bored of the daily grind. Instead, it gave daily life energy. Only by being close to him and knowing that she could do what she had to do whenever she put her mind to it made it possible for her to live a normal life.

It was fun working at the store. She especially liked pointing the scanner at items and seeing a number come up, then pointing it again and getting the total. Coincidence never meddled; logic was not required. Sometimes the barcode wouldn't scan and she had to input the number by hand, or cancel out an order and redo it because of a minor glitch, but other than that, nothing unexpected ever happened.

Her favorite part was getting to see the things that customers brought to the register or ordered over the phone. She memorized all of it: which types of fruit, yogurt, or instant foods sold the most, which brand of gum or gummy candy they grabbed on impulse while waiting at the register, which batteries, which fresh foods, which detergents, which bottled waters. The grocery store register informed her that daily life was a process of consuming one small product after another.

For the past few years, Se-oh had not once comparison-shopped at different stores to get a better deal. She hadn't stood in line for over thirty minutes at a government office or wandered from department to department in search of someone who could help her. She hadn't argued with salespeople who refused to give her a refund or called customer service to schedule after-sales service, and then called again to confirm the appointment and pleaded for their technician to show up on time. Her father had done all of that. Se-oh had stayed home and avoided daily life. Of course, not everything about working at the grocery store was good. Sometimes she saw people whose faces resembled those of people she once knew. Still others, who looked like no one that she knew, would stare at her and make her nervous. Her face would flush, her hands would tremble. She was certain they would shout her name at any moment. But it never happened. They simply stared at her as they handed her their credit card or waited for her to make change.

When she summoned the courage to steal peeks at customers' faces, she was consumed by pointless thoughts. Such as, how old was that face looking back at her? She herself was the only person whose exact age she knew. When she looked at her own reflection, she thought, Is this really a twenty-seven-year-old face? Not fat, but bloated. Exuding dissatisfaction, as if it had suffered some injustice. The corners of the lips drawn down, angry looking, and the rest of the mouth following suit, deepening the marionette lines. Eyelids that drooped even when she wasn't tired, making her look sleepy and bored.

If hers was a typical twenty-seven-year-old face, then was Su-ho's a typical twenty-nine-year-old's? And if so, did that mean Se-oh would soon wear the same face—tired and dull, yet somehow also neurotic and so utterly dripping with victim mentality that he looked like a dog with its tail between its legs?

Se-oh often wondered, as she watched people choose between different items, what they were doing back when they'd turned twenty. How did they make it through their twenties that they should now be in this store, picking out bottled water and spinach and purchasing instant rice?

From there, she would find herself thinking about Mi-yeon Cho. In fact, she never really stopped thinking about her. There were simply times when thoughts of her floated right at the surface, and times when they didn't. Where was she now, and was she living this kind of life? When did it become possible for her? How long did it take for her to be able to converse comfortably with others again?

Talking to Jae-hyung and Wu-sul made Se-oh acutely aware of just how much her own conversational skills had slipped. She'd had no problem talking to her father. While hiding at home, she'd watched a lot of TV dramas, news, and variety shows. She'd stayed on top of online trends. Sometimes, without even meaning to, she'd found that she knew all there was to know about some newsworthy incident. But real-life conversations were different from what you saw on TV or read online. She never blanked on any words, and yet she couldn't seem to carry a conversation.

The problem wasn't that she'd forgotten how to talk to people or what an appropriate topic of conversation was. It was that when she saw her two coworkers, she realized she was in no position to socialize. Her face went straight in reaction to jokes, and when she tried to laugh, she turned brusque instead. Talking unreservedly, with no regards to the future, filled her with guilt. And thinking about what happened to Su-ho every day in her imagination made her fear becoming friends with her coworkers.

They lived in a completely different world from hers. The world of human beings with good intentions. But the thing about human beings was that the moment you let yourself get carried away with thinking people were essentially good at heart, they would prove you wrong. They would make comments at your expense, cut you down casually like it meant nothing to them, then laugh for no reason, and when your mood turned foul and you complained, they would suddenly have your back. Given that, human beings couldn't care less about the line between good and evil.

When Se-oh looked at it that way, she wanted to turn herself over body and soul to the tiny grocery store. She wanted to live a life of small happinesses, little joys that came from knowing that not all relationships were based on people setting traps for each other, or being tied to each other in a brutal food chain, or harboring grudges and fury, but rather they could be based on discovering yourself through joyful work, through trying new things, and by conversing and joking with people you had the privilege of calling your coworkers.

A vain hope. It was too late for her. For starters, the malice she carried was not going anywhere. It ate away at her from the inside. Each time she thought about Su-ho, she was instantly returned to a world of wounds and lies and death and anger, a place of constant threats and mockery and violence and sarcasm. It was not just Su-ho's world. Se-oh had already familiarized herself with it. It had been her world too, once.

17

The events of those days had a way of coming back to her at random moments. It got worse after she started following Su-ho. After all, part of her job back then was to keep a watchful eye on others.

Back then. When she could do anything she wanted and yet could do nothing at all. When she wanted to get away but didn't know where to go, and when the place she got away to only became another place she would have to escape. When day and night, summer and winter, today and tomorrow were all the same. Looking back on it now, nothing had really changed since then. She'd been so clueless. Thinking that the worst part of her life had passed. She'd had no idea she would make it through hell only to have to step back down into the muck again in order to get through the next hell.

Now that she'd stopped hiding out at home, Se-oh kept coming across people who looked like Mi-yeon. Women with similar slim physiques and the kind of faint smile that came off as standoffish but that those close to her knew was genuine. Women with thick, black hair down to their shoulders, who styled themselves in clothing and handbags that looked simple but had been crafted with great care and attention to detail. For all of Mi-yeon's apparent uniqueness, it turned out there were a lot of women like her.

Se-oh froze each time she saw one. She would get flustered, trip over her own feet, draw attention to herself. She would rush ahead and openly examine the woman's face. Her mind would not rest until she'd confirmed it was not Mi-yeon. At the same time, it angered her that Mi-yeon still hadn't surfaced. She realized that her conflicting emotions were allowing "back then" to continue its grip on the present.

Se-oh and Mi-yeon had once been best friends. In fact, they were more like family, having practically grown up together. They could tell each other anything. Se-oh had no other friend who listened to her without judgment. Mi-yeon alone did that for her. Se-oh could say anything without fear of being misunderstood. They talked endlessly every chance they got, sharing everything the moment they were alone together, until they both knew everything there was to know about each other.

Back then Se-oh had a habit of stroking Mi-yeon's earlobe. Whenever her finger touched that soft, scarred lobe, Mi-yeon's lips would part slightly. While in the middle of talking or listening, Se-oh would watch closely until Mi-yeon exhaled. Each time her breath brushed Se-oh's skin, she felt a stirring in some unknown place.

In elementary school, Mi-yeon had had her ears pierced and started wearing glittery, cubic zirconia earrings. Se-oh never touched Mi-yeon's earlobes when she wore the earrings. The earlobes looked like they were a part of the accessory. As Se-oh and Mi-yeon moved up to middle school, the dress code grew stricter, and Mi-yeon had to take the earrings out. The holes closed up, leaving behind a small knob of scar tissue, as if to show that no injury can ever heal to its original state.

Their other friends were shocked to see Se-oh massaging Mi-yeon's earlobes or delicately stroking her eyelashes. But Se-oh refused to stop doing these things that she alone was allowed to do.

Things began to change after they started high school. At first Se-oh thought it was because they had less free time. They attended different schools, which meant there was far more catching up to do each time they talked. They even had to tell each other what color their gym clothes were. Se-oh hoped that Mi-yeon would tell her everything and not leave a single thing out, but she soon realized it was impossible. She didn't know how it was for Mi-yeon, but for Se-oh, it was time-consuming work. She had to accept that they could not return to their previous state of perfect knowledge.

To make matters worse, Mi-yeon not only stopped talking about herself, she stopped having time to listen to Se-oh. During their phone conversations, Se-oh could hear Mi-yeon clacking away at something. Mi-yeon gave formulaic responses, and when Se-oh asked her opinion or sought her agreement, Mi-yeon deflected the question to hide the fact that she hadn't been listening. When they met in person, if Se-oh reached for her earlobe, Mi-yeon's face would turn hard and she would pull away. She never told Se-oh to stop, but her face never softened either. Se-oh pretended not to notice. Mi-yeon's aloofness and attitude were a part of the person that Se-oh liked.

Not that Se-oh told her everything. It worried her greatly that Mi-yeon was gradually changing, but some topics of conversation become decisive the moment they are broached. This topic was one of them.

As they'd grown older, Mi-yeon's tendencies toward callousness and fickleness had grown worse. She could be kind and friendly when she wanted to, but mostly she was aloof. Se-oh sometimes felt she was trying too hard to please Mi-yeon. She could tell it would become too much for her one day. She used to think she knew Mi-yeon well, but that had all changed. Whenever she wanted to feel superior to Mi-yeon, or when she felt frustrated at the lack of a reward for her continued loyalty, Se-oh told herself it was because her friend had grown up without a father, and she felt sorry for her. But it made her extremely angry when Mi-yeon blamed Se-oh's excessive attachment to her on Se-oh's lack of a mother.

She found she spent more and more time waiting in silence for Mi-yeon to say something. She even stopped reaching for Mi-yeon's earlobes. They usually met at a playground about halfway between their houses, where they would sit on a bench or quietly swing on the swings. As she became conscious of the silence, Se-oh found it harder to look at an empty swing set, a seesaw with one end tipped high into the air, a jungle gym with no one climbing on it, a rusted slide.

What had become of the stories they used to share? She'd thought they were etched into each other's bodies, as indelible as veins. But no. Their stories had plunged into a deep crevasse in the earth. They'd fallen to the bottom of a frigid ravine. They'd vanished into a pitch-dark cave.

Se-oh tried to imagine how Mi-yeon spent her time. She had a lot of time to herself, just like Se-oh. She had to. The alternative was impossible. What they did with that time and the things they thought about were surely different, just as the intervals between their breaths and the way they drew air into their lungs were also different from each other. Just as their shadows belonged to them alone, they each had a space and a time all their own. Why had it taken Se-oh so long to realize it? She'd stupidly mistaken attachment and obsession for friendship. She was ashamed.

But even after realizing it, she did not give up on this friendship that was hers alone. She felt she had to be selfless and put Mi-yeon first. The more she did so, the more her unbearable sense of shame hardened and grew more secretive.

The person who killed her hope that things would get better with time was Bu-wi. He went to the same high school as Mi-yeon. As he began appearing more frequently in Mi-yeon's stories, Se-oh's spirits fell. The first time Mi-yeon told her about him, she'd bubbled with excitement. She'd gone on and on about whatever uninteresting mischief he'd gotten into and giggled stupidly. She retold the same trivial details over and over. Then she started to say something more, but stopped and refused to finish no matter how much Se-oh badgered her. Se-oh had assumed it was something else about Bu-wi.

Mi-yeon seemed to be in awe of Bu-wi. She talked about how witty and generous and thoughtful and kind he was. Whenever she talked about the things he liked, she sounded just as excited as when she talked about the things she liked.

Se-oh had seen Bu-wi once. At an after-school cram class. Mi-yeon had tried to act uninterested in Bu-wi while Se-oh was around. Se-oh was the only one who knew Mi-yeon wasn't acting like herself, and she couldn't help being conscious of it.

Se-oh didn't care for Bu-wi at all. To put it bluntly, she was closer to hating him. So much so that she felt disappointed in Mi-yeon for choosing to be friends with him. Bu-wi was far too rambunctious. It was like he couldn't bear to be bored for even a second. And he was always cracking terrible jokes. Plus, he didn't exactly seem to be in love with Mi-yeon. That, at least, was fortunate.

Once, on a day off from school, Se-oh ran into Bu-wi on the bus. Bu-wi greeted her first.

"What are you doing alone? You and Mi-yeon are usually joined at the hip."

It made Se-oh happy to hear that.

"Oh, that's right," he added, "Mi-yeon said she had plans today."

And just like that, Se-oh's good mood was ruined. Mi-yeon hadn't told her about any plans.

It hadn't come up during their phone call the night before. Se-oh grew quiet because of what Bu-wi told her and because of what she was guessing. Instead of asking where Mi-yeon was, she asked Bu-wi where he was going.

"Church."

He kept his answer short and turned to look out the bus window. Se-oh thought he was feigning seriousness, but it turned out that Bu-wi simply had nothing else to say on the subject. Se-oh felt irritated. It took great effort for her to tell herself that befriending Bu-wi, with Mi-yeon in the middle, was to her advantage. Not that he shared any such interest.

"I like your T-shirt. That design looks good on you," she said.

"You think so?" he said, sounding reluctant.

Se-oh suspected she should not ask anything more, but there was something she wanted to know.

"Where'd you buy it?"

Bu-wi seemed to know that Se-oh wasn't actually interested in his T-shirt. He shrugged and didn't respond.

"I only ask because it's an unusual print."

The T-shirt sported a large, colorful print of an owl. She would have said the same thing if it were a zebra or a tiger instead. It wouldn't have made a difference if there were no design at all. Bu-wi laughed. She wasn't sure why.

"Why are you laughing?" Se-oh asked, careful to keep her voice friendly. If she sounded like she was prying, he would get secretive.

"Because. You and Mi-yeon are so alike."

Now he was showing off. He knew she was digging for information, and he wanted to lord the information over her. Like all the other pretentious, boring kids would do.

She couldn't imagine what Bu-wi and Mi-yeon might have talked about that would make him say that. What did he know about Mi-yeon? Could he really have talked to her enough to be able to say they had the same personalities or tastes or ways of speaking? What on earth had Mi-yeon told him?

Bu-wi shocked her by acting like he knew Mi-yeon well. Se-oh tried to think of a way to put her mind at ease. She wanted to tell him something that Mi-yeon didn't know. Just like Mi-yeon, she wanted to have secrets, too. Secrets that would hold for a little while but that she wouldn't be able to keep forever.

Se-oh started going to church again. The same church Bu-wi attended. Bu-wi wasn't loose-lipped or prone to bragging. But he would let the news slip eventually. Because it wasn't something he would even think of keeping secret.

The third time she went to his church, Se-oh gave Bu-wi a watch. It was a sports watch, a style hugely popular among kids their age. She'd spent all of her savings to buy it for Mi-yeon.

She chose to give it to him right before the service began. The other kids wouldn't crowd around to check out his gift, but there also wouldn't be zero witnesses either.

"What's this?"

Bu-wi turned the box this way and that, as if the answer were written on the wrapping paper.

"A present."

"I can see that, but why are you giving it to me?"

He didn't look happy about the surprise gift. He gave no indication of appreciation and made no move to unwrap it.

"It's for your birthday."

"Do you mean the birthday that's four months from now, or the one that happened eight months ago?"

Se-oh couldn't tell from his tone whether he was liking this or not.

"Both. Happy belated birthday and happy upcoming birthday."

"My own family barely celebrates it, so I don't know why you would celebrate two of them at once."

Now she knew. He hated it. He might even make her take the gift back.

"It's no fun to do it at the same time as everyone else."

Bu-wi's face softened a little at that. He looked like he was even starting to enjoy the surprise. He hesitated a moment longer and then said thanks. Se-oh liked that. She liked that he hesitated, and she liked that he gave in and accepted the gift.

"Aren't you going to open it?"

"I'll open it later."

She figured he simply couldn't be bothered. He turned to rush into the chapel. Se-oh grabbed his arm.

"Don't tell anyone."

"Huh?"

"Don't tell anyone I gave you a present."

Bu-wi turned back and faced her straight on.

"Who are you telling me to keep it a secret from?"

"Everyone. You can't tell anyone."

"I'm not okay with that. I'll just give it back to you."

"Please take it. It's yours."

Se-oh kept her voice earnest and shy. That would give the secret more value. The heavier the secret, the more certain it would leak out.

"Take it back, and I promise not to tell anyone you tried to give it to me."

Bu-wi pressed the box into her hand and turned and went into the chapel. Se-oh fought back tears. She tried to think only about the secret that had just been born regardless of whether he went along with it. At last, she'd hatched a secret, and yet she felt terrible.

Before long, she could sense the other kids at the cram school whispering about her.

No sooner did Se-oh ask one of her friends about it than the girl jumped right in, as if she'd been waiting for just that moment.

"I don't know if I should tell you this, but . . ." Few stories that began with that phrase were worth suffering through, but Se-oh endured. She already knew the other kids weren't exactly crazy about her. She wasn't a great student, didn't have much of a personality, and was always tagging along after Mi-yeon. So whatever it was the girl was pretending to be reluctant to say had to be about Se-oh or Mi-yeon.

And she was right. The girl left out parts in order to avoid naming names, but it was clearly about Se-oh. The gossip included what Se-oh really had said and done to Bu-wi. She figured the parts about what Bu-wi and Mi-yeon said and did also included some truths. But in the end, most of it turned out to be overblown or embellished. Even Se-oh herself couldn't tell which parts were true and which were made up.

She should have set the girl straight, but she feigned ignorance instead. Trying didn't mean things would go her way. And anyway, those sorts of rumors never just cropped up without reason. She simply had to wait it out. Of course, Se-oh wasn't worried about rumors spreading. What worried her was that, as the story made its rounds, certain parts would get exaggerated to the point that none of it would be believable.

It would make its way around to Mi-yeon eventually. Even if she didn't hear what they were whispering about, she would figure it out from their attitudes. She would find out about it belatedly and want to claim that it was all exaggerated or untrue, but she would refrain, since some of it was true. According to the gossip, Mi-yeon was the instigator among the three of them. It didn't cast her in a positive light.

The two of them never talked about him. They kept their mouths shut about the rumors, including the parts that could have used airing out. But they still saw each other now and then, and pretended nothing was amiss. Whenever a subject arose that they were better off avoiding, they either didn't talk about it at all or only discussed part of it. As a result, Se-oh felt like Bu-wi was constantly with them.

One evening, Se-oh was sitting by herself at the playground when someone appeared at her side. It was Mi-yeon. Se-oh did not turn to look at her, and Mi-yeon did not greet her. After a while, Se-oh addressed Mi-yeon first.

"What do you have to say for yourself?"

"I thought maybe you had something you wanted to say to me."

Mi-yeon's voice was gentle, unlike Se-oh's sharp tone. She

even gave her a little smile. Albeit a distant one. Se-oh didn't respond. She was beginning to understand, however faintly, the power that greed and jealousy could wield over an ordinary friendship, and how easy it was to completely distort a relationship.

That was as far as it went. The two of them sat quietly for a while. The words spilling out of her throat stayed pooled inside Se-oh's mouth. They were as heavy as if she'd swallowed iron. She wanted to confess. Her jealousy, Mi-yeon's coldness, the unnatural tension that Bu-wi had placed between them. The watch she'd tried to give Bu-wi. The rumors she'd purposely started.

In that silence, Se-oh came to the clear realization that she alone had ruined their friendship. She wanted to prove to Mi-yeon that she was willing to do anything for her. She wanted to profess her unchanging love and apologize for all that had happened. The overwhelming desire to touch Mi-yeon's earlobe the way she had when they were kids tormented her. But she suppressed it. Instead she tapped her finger restlessly against her thigh.

It flustered Se-oh to realize that she'd never imagined this situation arising. It filled her with regret, just like when she'd first realized her own stupidity. It would not be easy to get over.

18

Their first phone call in three years. Should she have been suspicious from the get-go? That is, should she have known something was fishy the moment Mi-yeon said her name warmly, remarked on how it had been far too long since she'd last called, and said, "So what've you been up to?" as if it had only been three days and not three years?

Se-oh hesitated when she realized it was Mi-yeon. Instead of answering the question, she said, "How've you been?"

"A little busy, but enjoying life." Mi-yeon sounded breezy. "Where are you, Se-oh? At home?"

"Yeah."

It was her fourth semester break since starting college. Her father was in the middle of closing up his tool and die shop, which had been in the red since taking a big hit during the push for commercial redevelopment. It was obvious that he'd be left with debt after the business closed. For all she knew, she would probably have to take a leave of absence the next semester.

"Where are you?" she asked Mi-yeon.

"I'm taking a break from school to work. It was an opportunity

141

I couldn't pass up. You know how hard it is to find a job these days. I got lucky."

Unlike Se-oh, who felt awkward and unsure of what to say, Mi-yeon sounded cheerful, as if implying they merely had to get past this moment.

"We should meet up some time, don't you think?" Mi-yeon said.

She sounded as casual as if she were asking Se-oh what she'd had for lunch or if she'd seen the news of the latest celebrity scandal.

Se-oh was quiet for a moment while she gathered her thoughts. Over the phone, she heard someone in the background calling Mi-yeon's name. Mi-yeon's voice was faint as she replied, "Yes, ma'am. I'll be right there."

"Se-oh, I'm really sorry but the team leader needs to see me right now. We have to go over something. I'm sorry to hang up so quickly. Can I call you back later?"

Se-oh nodded, then remembered she was on the phone and said, "Sure, call me back later." It had shocked her to hear Mi-yeon say sorry. And "really sorry," at that. The old Mi-yeon would never have apologized for anything.

If she hadn't called back, Se-oh would have chalked the whole thing up to one of Mi-yeon's sudden change of moods. But, as if to prove she'd meant what she said, Mi-yeon called back and told Se-oh when and where to meet her. In that respect, she wasn't so different after all. She'd decided on the time and place without bothering to ask for Se-oh's opinion. It was good to see that she was the same as ever. Other than sounding friendlier and more considerate, that is, as if conscious of the fact that they were no longer close.

Se-oh couldn't help feeling a little excited. She'd even ditched her father, who kept heaving deep sighs while cleaning out his shop, to go shopping for a new outfit. On the way to Gangnam Station, she got a call from Mi-yeon telling her to meet near Gyodae Station instead. Sounding excessively polite, Mi-yeon apologized several times for inconveniencing her. Se-oh had a weird feeling about it. The old Mi-yeon would never have apologized for switching locations at the last minute, since she would have had good reason for doing so. Se-oh had never criticized Mi-yeon for being inconsiderate. Their relationship was such that they could give each other that kind of slack.

She was changing trains to head for Gyodae Station when it occurred to her to wonder why Mi-yeon had called her for the first time in three years right in the middle of the workday. If it were Se-oh, she would have waited until after work, when she was home alone for the rest of the night with nothing else to do. Night was when your loneliness enticed you, gave you the courage to contact someone out of the blue.

What kind of day was Mi-yeon having that she suddenly thought of Se-oh while at work? Especially work that was urgent enough for her team leader to come looking for her. Se-oh felt glum. It must have been something very trivial, something she would never guess at, that made Mi-yeon think of Se-oh and decide to call her on impulse. She could only assume Mi-yeon had deliberately chosen a busy time to call in order to avoid addressing the heavy and difficult question of why they hadn't spoken in so long.

With her mind pinballing from thought to thought, she got off the train. She wanted to go around to the opposite platform and head right back in the other direction. As if guessing Se-oh might be feeling that way, Mi-yeon called just then to ask if Se-oh was almost there. The whole sequence of events, from Mi-yeon inviting her out to changing the location and then checking to see if she was on her way, left Se-oh feeling that Mi-yeon was a little desperate to see her. This wasn't consideration; Mi-yeon was anxious about something. Se-oh didn't know why, but Mi-yeon was going out of her way to stay on Se-oh's good side.

Mi-yeon arrived a few minutes late and headed straight for Se-oh with a big smile spread across her face. Se-oh smiled back. She wasn't used to being greeted with such enthusiasm. Mi-yeon's voice had a shrill note of excitement to it, such that Se-oh felt bad for having been suspicious of her.

Mi-yeon had lost quite a bit of weight. She looked tired, but she also had the respectable, credible air of someone with a good office job. Like two old friends seeing each other after a long time apart, they asked what was new, where they lived now, how their families were. Even while asking questions and giving her own short answers, Mi-yeon kept looking around and glancing back at the entrance. When she saw that Se-oh was staring at her, she hurriedly smiled and made an effort to soften her face. Once they ran out of the easy conversation topics, Mi-yeon let out a deep sigh. Then she began talking about how she was making good money at her job. She launched so seamlessly into one work anecdote after another that Se-oh could hardly get a word in edgewise. Se-oh assumed she kept talking about work out of the awkwardness of meeting after such a long time. If not for Mi-yeon, Se-oh probably would have done the same, latching on to any random topic that came to mind. In fact, she had worried that their conversation might hit an awkward lull and that Mi-yeon would get bored and regret having called her.

After talking at length about her job, Mi-yeon finally asked, "How's your father's store doing? I heard that all of those places have been going under lately." Se-oh felt suddenly like she'd been talking to a perfect stranger all along. It was inconsiderate and downright rude of Mi-yeon.

To what extent was she still the Mi-yeon that Se-oh had known? At what point had she stopped being a friend? The old Mi-yeon had been cold and unpredictable, but also discreet and thoughtful. Even while seemingly indifferent, she could be considerate in subtle ways.

But not anymore. The longer they spoke, the more sarcastic she seemed. She smiled but didn't look like she was enjoying herself. Her exaggerated small talk was not due to awkwardness; she was trying to hide something.

Each time Mi-yeon paused for even a second, it was to glance around or look at her watch or check her cell phone. Se-oh needed to say something. Otherwise the silence would expose the fact that their friendship had long been over. She kept belatedly tacking on comments to whatever Mi-yeon said and asking the same questions that Mi-yeon had asked her. When did she move, was her job hard, when did she plan to return to school? Questions that made plain how long it had been since they last saw each other.

Mi-yeon answered each question brusquely and then suddenly turned serious.

"Let's get dinner now."

She sprang up and headed straight out of the café. It was a little early for dinner, but Se-oh followed. Se-oh paid for the coffee and joined Mi-yeon outside. Mi-yeon was on the phone with someone.

"What should we eat?" Se-oh asked, after waiting for her to hang up.

Mi-yeon ignored the question and started walking. Se-oh followed. She couldn't see her face very well while walking beside her, but the look in Mi-yeon's eyes had darkened noticeably since leaving the café.

"Let's go there."

Mi-yeon took her to an ox-bone soup place not far from the café. Considering how quickly she headed for it, Mi-yeon seemed to have had it in mind already.

Se-oh wrapped her hands around the bowl of soup with its milky-white broth that the waitress had set in front of her. She had the brief thought that this was the first time she and Mi-yeon had gone out for soup together. And it was proving to be a disappointment. A very unmemorable first. Their reunion was as bland as the broth.

Mi-yeon worked on her soup without saying a word. She was completely different from how she'd been in the café. She put down her spoon and stared at Se-oh.

"Se-oh," she said finally, "the truth is . . ."

Se-oh swallowed her mouthful of broth and waited to hear what Mi-yeon was about to say. The soup had already cooled, but it seemed to scald her throat. Her face flushed, and her whole body grew hot. It scared her to think that none other than Mi-yeon was having this effect on her.

Mi-yeon's eyes were as big and dark as ever. Those eyes had once bewitched Se-oh. Each time she'd looked at her, they'd sparkled. Now her eyes were different, but they were still bewitching. Se-oh stared into them for a long time before realizing they held a completely different allure than before. She wasn't sure just what it was. Se-oh's face must have hardened, because Mi-yeon cracked a tiny smile. It was an impeccably natural smile. The more natural she thought it looked, the more Mi-yeon's face seemed to darken with a certain ruthlessness. If there was such a thing as a face that had been eaten away by life, this was it.

19

The morning after Se-oh withdrew the cash from the ATM and
counted it over and over, Mi-yeon disappeared. She didn't show
up for the 6:00 a.m. assembly. Maybe she'd just stepped away for
a moment. Maybe she was using the toilet. Maybe she'd woken
early and gone for a walk, or popped out to buy some missing
ingredients in the middle of preparing breakfast. Despite all of
those possibilities, Se-oh knew that Mi-yeon had simply left. It
wasn't a guess so much as a conviction.

Se-oh had woken to the sound of voices. Each time she woke
up in that room, it alarmed her to realize she was lying next to
strangers. The different densities of darkness kept bleeding into
each other only to redefine themselves the next moment as Se-oh
marveled repeatedly at where she was. Later, she lay in a faint,
almost colorless light and thought about nothing at all. She could
see the dark brown molding that edged the ceiling, but she could
not make out the pattern on the ceiling. Patterns kept shrinking
down and growing large again.

The walls were empty. There was nothing strange about that.
As recently as yesterday, Mi-yeon had dozed off leaning against

the wall next to Se-oh. Now Mi-yeon could rest easy. Five million won had made sure of that. Se-oh had lied to her father to get that money.

There were two rooms facing each other, with a combination living room and kitchen in between as narrow as a hallway. Those who'd already woken up were gathered there and whispering to each other, clearly trying to keep something secret. As others joined them, the whispering grew louder.

"Mi-yeon will be working with a different team starting today," their team leader said, even before Se-oh could ask about her.

The look of curiosity in everyone's eyes dimmed. The ensuing silence made Se-oh lonely. If they'd kept whispering instead, she wouldn't have felt so alienated, so left out of the open secret.

She walked next to the team leader on the way to the training center. Fortunately, the team leader did not loop her arm through Se-oh's this time. Instead, she was staring off into space absent-mindedly, in stark contrast to the friendly demeanor she'd maintained up until yesterday.

"Can I tell you something?"

Se-oh figured it was going to be another example of a success story. The same stuff she'd been hearing throughout her training.

"We had a team member once who tried to run away. She only made it as far as a nearby convenience store. She had nowhere else to go, and it was the only place open at that hour. She stepped through the door and screamed at the cashier. She must have been feeling very desperate. I don't know what she had to feel so desperate about, but then again, the thought of running away itself ought to make anyone pretty desperate. They said she yelled like crazy, 'Help me! Save me!'"

The team leader's impression was so realistic that for a moment it sounded like she really was begging for help. It clearly wasn't the first time she'd told that story.

"What do you think the cashier did?"

The team leader stopped short and looked at Se-oh. She waited, as if to give Se-oh time to think about her answer. Then she continued.

"He yawned. A great, big yawn, like this. His shift was almost up and he must've been exhausted. Finally, he said, 'What? You were locked up, too?'"

The team leader laughed and resumed walking.

"The escaped team member begged the cashier to loan her his cell phone. As you know, the team leaders confiscate everyone's phones. You couldn't even call the police if you wanted to. But the cashier wouldn't loan her his phone. It was brand-new, the latest model. You can't loan just anyone your brand-new phone. It'll get stolen. You know the type. They ask if they can use your phone for a second and then they take off with it. Of course he didn't dare. So the team member begged him to at least call the police for her. She kept staring out the window like someone was after her. The cashier had no choice but to call the police. Instead of telling them that someone was asking for help, he reported a strange person loitering inside the store. While waiting for the police to arrive, the team member hid behind the trash can, even though no one came looking for her. You know how they have separate trash cans in the convenience stores for dumping the left-over broth from instant noodle cups? The ones that smell and have bits of soggy, discarded ramen stuck to the floor around them? Yeah, she was hiding behind that. And each time someone came in, she ducked between the shelves. The cashier kept staring at her, annoyed, and then finally yelled at her to stop messing with the displays. Each time, the team member cowered and apologized over and over. She refused to leave. After twenty minutes or so, a police officer arrived. Taking his sweet time. He opened the door with no sense of urgency whatsoever and said, 'Someone call for the police?' The team member sprang out from hiding and hugged him as if it were her mother herself. The officer brushed her off in annoyance and said, 'The pyramid? Not that place again.' There were so many others like her, you see. But do you know what ended up happening to that girl?"

The team leader stopped again, suddenly dropping her polite register. She said nothing for a moment before resuming walking. She wasn't doing it to give Se-oh time to think. She was telling her to imagine the future of a runaway whom even the police wouldn't help.

"She came back a week later. Makes sense when you think about it. She would have learned the hard way that the world never gives losers a second chance. No one would have helped her. She realized the only way to succeed was to make her own opportunities. By that, I mean working really hard to succeed here, in this place. Because, here, opportunities are given out fairly. It's the only truly democratic place in the whole world. That person, by the way, was me."

Se-oh was hardly surprised. She nodded without saying anything. The five days of training she'd received so far had been pretty effective. If you went along with it, more or less, then the work wasn't too hard to do. It had a way of disarming people, allowing you to get what you wanted. What Se-oh wanted right now was for the team leader to stop talking.

She seemed to be saying that Mi-yeon would return eventually.

She knew that was what Se-oh wanted to hear. Mi-yeon had to come back. She had to come back and apologize. Even if it was nothing more than the pricks of a guilty conscience that brought her back. Even if it had nothing whatsoever to do with the long, deep friendship they'd once shared.

It was also a warning to Se-oh that there was no point in trying to run. Why think about escaping when you could think about succeeding instead? Se-oh stayed, though not because of the team leader's story. She worked hard and used what she'd learned from the manual and the training she'd received from the team leader.

She thought often about Mi-yeon. But she thought even more about herself, stuck there on her own. Thinking about Mi-yeon only left her feeling depressed at the thought that Mi-yeon would never return. Thinking about herself at least helped her to understand to some extent why Mi-yeon didn't come back.

After Mi-yeon ran away, Se-oh fell into the habit of listening for someone sneaking up behind her. She would leave the dorm in the morning feeling no hope at all, but upon returning after work, the thought that Mi-yeon might be there gave her a tiny bit of strength. She even spent whole days waiting in stupid anticipation for Mi-yeon.

A week passed. Mi-yeon did not return. Coming back was the sort of thing that only happened to people like the team leader or the other team members. It did not happen to someone like Mi-yeon, who would never, ever look back once she'd started walking away. Despite how badly Se-oh wanted to deny it, the fact remained: Mi-yeon had not changed in the slightest.

She hated Mi-yeon. She hated her as much as she'd once relied on her and befriended her. She didn't hate her for not returning Se-oh's friendship as she once had. She hated her for waiting until

Se-oh had become a full-fledged member, when they could have left together instead. She hated her for choosing Se-oh as her final recruit before disappearing. For leaving her behind when she ran away. Above all, she hated her for not telling Se-oh that she was planning to escape. Just as she had in the past, Mi-yeon had kept her secrets from Se-oh.

Se-oh began working in earnest. To keep the friends she called up from realizing how broke she was, she kept her voice cheerful and spoke clearly and with confidence. At first, she focused on those she thought she could rely on the most. Later, she contacted people she had at least some acquaintance with. She called people she hadn't spoken to in years, old high school classmates whose names she barely remembered, people she'd gone to elementary school with, middle school classmates who'd gone to the same church, and college classmates she'd spoken to once or twice. The most effective networks were the ones like Se-oh and Mi-yeon's relationship. That is, friends who were once special to each other but had since fallen out of touch.

With each number she called, she feared being turned down. But after experiencing it enough times, she began to take it in stride. She relied on the team leader's instructions that if you only called ten people, you would be turned down ten times, but if you called a hundred people, then at least twenty of them would hear you out. She had no choice but to place call after call. It shamed her at first to think that she was involved in something shady, but those thoughts gradually faded. Despite what they thought, she was not begging for money or luring them into guaranteed failure. She was simply teaching them about a special opportunity that would enable them to choose their future.

She kept on contacting people she barely knew, was rejected each time, and met others in person only to return humiliated. It didn't happen often, but now and then she would convince someone she knew to spend five days in the dorm, just as Se-oh had, after which they would deposit five million won to change their status from recruit to team member. Friends who began doing business under Se-oh brought in other friends. Later they attacked Se-oh, cursed her, and left together. Family members of those she'd recruited came to the dorm, too, to physically accost Se-oh, grabbing her by the collar and shoving her around. She would shout back, shove them to the ground, with no clue of what it was she was really trying to protect, and cling to her downline to try to keep them from leaving. But in the end, they all left.

At first she stayed in order to wait for Mi-yeon. Later, she couldn't leave because of the money she'd squandered and her steadily mounting debt. She'd wanted consolation for Mi-yeon's betrayal, but soon enough she needed five million won and more. Though, if she were honest about it, the five million had always been more important than Mi-yeon. Se-oh had been in no position to spend it so carelessly. Five million needed to turn into fifteen million, and then into fifty million. The thought of making that much money in a single stroke drove her to take out a bank loan. More debt led to more and more loans. She repeated the process countless times, but that first five million won never found its way back to her.

Five million was an enormous amount. The fact that she could not manage to save it up was proof enough, as was the fact that it had confined her to that place for over a year and a half. The day she'd counted every bill of the five million won her father had transferred to her, the scent of cash lingered on her hands for a long time. Now the scent had vanished.

As her debts mounted, her contacts decreased. Before long,

she'd run through everyone she knew. She began dialing numbers at random. She was desperate for someone to at least pretend to recognize her name. She figured this was probably the point at which Mi-yeon had thought of her. She was sure she wasn't the first person on Mi-yeon's mind. But once Mi-yeon had thought of her, she would not have hesitated to call Se-oh. Just as Se-oh wouldn't now, either. What mattered was not friendship, or honor, or the value of relationships.

What mattered was five million won.

20

Every time Mi-yeon introduced Bu-wi to someone, she would tell them, "He was the captain of the baseball team." As if that were the most essential thing about him.

It was hard to tell from his voice over the phone whether Bu-wi was still living up to the title of captain. Se-oh was so preoccupied with thinking about it that she stumbled over her words and didn't follow the manual.

"Hi, do you, uh, remember me?"

"I'm sorry, who is this?"

"It's Se-oh. Se-oh Yun."

"Se-oh Yun? Oh yeah, of course, I remember you."

"You do?"

"You had a crush on me."

The team leader saw Se-oh's face go stiff and hurriedly drew a smiley face on a piece of paper. Se-oh forced the corners of her mouth to angle up as she responded.

"Oh, you knew about that?"

"I was just joking."

"But it's true."

"Anyway, what's up?"

Bu-wi didn't sound like he was smiling. But he wasn't short with her, either, which put her mind at ease.

"How have you been?" Se-oh asked.

The team leader drew a large X on the paper. That meant to stop asking questions. It was better to save listening to the other person for later. The team leader scribbled, *Tell him how well you're doing.*

"How's school going?" Se-oh asked as she turned away from the team leader, who crossed her arms in resignation and sat back in her chair.

"We haven't talked in years, and that's what you want to ask me? What about you? Still ugly? Still built like a dump truck?"

Bu-wi laughed. Se-oh laughed, too. This was fun. Their laughter made her want to see him. She asked Bu-wi the same question Mi-yeon had asked her.

"We should meet up some time, don't you think?"

Bu-wi immediately asked, "What on earth for?" Se-oh laughed at that as well. The team leader gave her a look of pity, as if to say she'd just blown five million won.

"Don't you want to see for yourself whether I'm still ugly?" she asked.

"Faces don't change that much. Oh, wait, unless you got plastic surgery?"

Se-oh laughed again. She didn't realize until later that Bu-wi wasn't really saying those things in jest, but she assumed in the moment that he just wanted to make her laugh.

At their meeting spot, half an hour went by without any contact from Bu-wi. Se-oh started to dial his number but gave up. She figured she was being stood up. Willingly answering her call and joking around was one thing, but he had no real reason to meet her in person.

Thinking he wouldn't show made her more eager to see him. For all she knew, he might have caught word about her already. The friends who'd joined her in the training center had all gone back and quickly spread the word about her to others. Se-oh was learning that this work meant first losing your close friends, then losing the people you'd thought of as friends, and finally losing everyone.

She often tried to picture what Mi-yeon was doing, what kind of job she had, who she hung out with, and what she talked about after having left. It was as difficult as imagining the Mi-yeon who'd been in the pyramid. The Mi-yeon she'd seen for the first time in three years had broken into a dazzling smile at the sight of five million won; now she didn't know what might make Mi-yeon smile.

The minutes passed, and the likelihood of Bu-wi showing dwindled to nothing. It was time to give up. She didn't want to go back to the training center or to the dorm, but she could see the team leader waiting for her outside the coffee shop. Just as she was about to get up and leave, Bu-wi came running in. She was so happy to see him that she leapt out of her chair. Bu-wi waved at her. They'd always been on more formal terms before, but this time Se-oh followed suit and waved, too.

Bu-wi, with his broad shoulders, looked as strong and athletic as ever. The hand he'd waved at her looked thick and tanned, and he was breathing hard, as if he'd come running.

"Whaddya know? You *are* still ugly," he said.

Se-oh laughed hard. Bu-wi stared at her as if confused about why she was laughing.

They sat face to face but had nothing to talk about. Bu-wi grumbled about how the decor in the café made it look more like a children's petting zoo, and how the coffee was weak, and how it tasted like they'd just dipped the beans in warm water for a second. Se-oh stayed quiet, unsure of whether to bring up the past. Bu-wi seemed to be feeling the same way.

Then he surprised her by asking, "How's Mi-yeon?"

It was obvious from the question that Mi-yeon had never contacted Bu-wi to try to recruit him. He didn't know what had happened to her. Se-oh relaxed.

"I'm sure she's fine."

Bu-wi seemed to understand the implications of her answer. And yet they talked about Mi-yeon for a while anyway. She was the only thing they had in common.

She ended up telling him about how Mi-yeon used to give her the silent treatment when she was upset with her, and how she would rage at a shoelace that refused to tie easily or at someone who cut her off or walked too slowly in front of her on the sidewalk. And though Mi-yeon would nitpick at Se-oh for the most trivial things and render her speechless, she never snapped at her. On the other hand, when Mi-yeon herself did something wrong, she would act horribly indifferent. Se-oh would always apologize first simply to soften the mood. Then, right around the time it would be all but forgotten, Se-oh would show how hurt she was that Mi-yeon made her apologize first even though it was Mi-yeon's fault in the first place. Mi-yeon would give her a look as if disaster had just struck and explain to her convincingly of how emotionally exhausted Se-oh made her. Bu-wi remembered this aspect of Mi-yeon quite well, too.

Bu-wi was less talkative than she'd expected. Of course, that could have been because they'd never been close. He didn't say much about himself, but he didn't give the impression that he was hiding something or deliberately not talking. Nor did Se-oh get the feeling that he simply had nothing to say, or was keeping quiet because he had nothing worth sharing. He kept a polite distance, but didn't make that distance too obvious. He made Se-oh want to keep talking. He got her to open up and then listened carefully. He even nodded at all the right moments. She very nearly blurted out why she was really there and what Mi-yeon had done to her.

The team leader texted to tell her to take him to a second location. Se-oh rose and said goodbye to Bu-wi instead. She could have taken him somewhere else and brought up the pyramid, but she didn't. She didn't know why in the moment, but after returning to the drab dorm that night and seeing all those money-hungry team members seated in a circle, deep in the middle of a self-reflection session, she understood.

The thought of bringing him to the dorm filled her with shame. She didn't want him to see the tiny, cramped room, the groups of people sitting on the floor as they ate what passed for meals there, the piles of unsold merchandise stacked up all over the place, the bathroom with chunks of rotten food trapped in the drain cover.

She also realized after returning to the dorm that the clothes she wore were in terrible shape. She understood, too, how their cheap fabric and poor fit could make a person look so shabby. Her eyes were finally opened to the terribleness of the food that she only tolerated because she had no appetite anyway, and the unbearable discomfort of sleeping shoulder to shoulder with so many others every night.

Late that night, after the self-reflection session had ended and everyone was asleep, she lay there and thought about Bu-wi. The more she thought about him, the more she missed him. She wanted to tell him something. By the end of that long, sleepless night, she had thought of a way she could see him without feeling so ashamed. She would get him to join her here, after all.

Not long after, she met him again. Slowly, carefully, she talked about the constantly rising cost of tuition, the student loans that would take forever to pay off, the unclear career path that lay ahead of her after graduation, her choice of major that she wasn't cut out for. Bu-wi listened closely, chiming in now and then with his own woes.

When Bu-wi said he was hungry, Se-oh took him to a familiar restaurant without thinking too much about it. It was the restaurant she usually took prospective recruits to the first time they met. The same restaurant Mi-yeon had taken her to.

Two bowls of ox-bone soup came out. Now all she had to do was begin her pitch. It would be much harder than with anyone else. She took a big gulp of the broth first. It warmed her. Even if he turned this down, she was pretty sure he wouldn't say no to hanging out with her again.

"Bu-wi," she said slowly. She hesitated a moment, and then began by saying, "The truth is . . ." As she recited the lines she'd practiced the night before, Bu-wi ate spoonful after spoonful of his soup, the broth red from the spice paste he'd added.

After he'd polished off the bowl, Bu-wi sat quietly for a moment and then asked, "So how much have you made?"

Se-oh flinched. You can earn as much as you want. Your initial investment will become the seed that grows the tree that flowers with money. She was supposed to say the same abstract, figurative things that she said to everyone else. She couldn't tell him how much she'd made, because she hadn't made anything. All she'd done was steadily increase her debt. She was supposed to skirt the topic or respond by asking him how much he wanted to make. If she told him the truth, she would lose him. It didn't mean she was incompetent. With this type of work, you had to endure a period of failure and humiliation before you could succeed. Se-oh believed that firmly. And yet she couldn't bring herself to say any of it to Bu-wi.

Luckily, Bu-wi didn't seem interested in hearing her answer. He just muttered to himself, "Not that much, huh?" and let it drop. Unlike her other friends, he didn't criticize or make fun of Se-oh for falling for a scam. He didn't get angry or scorn her for trying to drag him into it, too. He didn't even accuse her of calling him under false pretenses. He didn't threaten her and tell her to never call him again. She was relieved. Now she had no reason to lie to him; she could drop the subterfuge.

When the team leader first handed her the "Action Guide" manual, she'd marveled at the contents. The manual categorized people according to different patterns of reactions. They may have all been individuals, but once they were in the manual, they became typical, collective beings.

Bu-wi was different. Especially the way he said, "I'll try it for the experience." And the way he said, "If it doesn't work out, let's quit together." And, "If neither you nor I can make a go of it, then that means it wasn't meant to be." And finally, "If you have trouble quitting, I'll help you."

She could have bluffed and said she was hardly in need of help. Worry about yourself, she could have said. She could have disparaged his good intentions and retorted, Who do you think you are to offer me help? She could have questioned his motives. Instead, she wanted to ask if she looked pathetic. She didn't, for fear it would sound stupid. She'd never feared that with anyone else before.

Se-oh stumbled on the way into the training center. Bu-wi told her to watch her step but did not take her hand or put an arm around her shoulders. He simply observed, his eyes devoid of affection or concern. He may as well have been looking at a sandwich board or a dog lying on the sidewalk.

A good four years had passed since that day, and yet Se-oh could still clearly recall the look in his eyes. It made her lose courage every time she started to miss him. But when she considered his indifferent yet cheerful voice, his thoughtful manner, and his calm, regular breaths, she thought maybe the lack of emotion he'd shown was forced. She even wondered at times if her guilt had driven her to imagine things. The thought began as a way to console herself, but later she believed it. She feared that, if she were ever to see him in person again, she might be shocked to learn that the look of perfect indifference had been real and not at all imagined as she hoped.

The four years she'd spent mulling over that look in his eyes had been a bumpy ride for her. Not that she was so naive as to think that time wasn't a rough and bumpy thing. She'd known it back then, too. She'd also known that the time she spent in the pyramid would be lopped off, severed from the rest of her life as if those months had never happened. But instead of being discarded and forgotten, they would weigh over her forever.

21

She had thought at first that the tenement flats were lush with plants and trees, an illusion created by the park that stood between her and them. With the park behind her now, the only greenery to be found was a single tree in the courtyard. From a distance, the black debris netting surrounding the demolition site had looked like a pit opening up beneath the buildings. Someone had slashed a warning, RESIDENTS ONLY, in bright red paint across the entrance.

The debris netting blocked out the sunlight, throwing the stairwell into darkness. And yet, outside, the weather was so clear she could see a cloud slowly drifting past, briefly caught in the frame of the window. The acrylic placard for the door number had fallen off, and in its place someone had written *101* with a marker. Se-oh Yun took a deep breath and rang the bell. The doorbell was black with grime except for the one spot in the center that had been rubbed bare by fingers. From the other side of the door, a voice asking who was there sounded very far away.

"I'm from the grocery store," Se-oh responded loudly.

She waited. Jae-hyung had warned her several times that she had to be patient with this one.

Inside the apartment, the old woman would be slowly making her way over, scooting across the floor on her butt. After a moment, Se-oh heard the knob turn. She stepped to one side. Slowly the door to #101 opened.

"You're from the grocery store?"

The voice came from below.

"Yes."

Se-oh stood straight and tall and examined the inside of the apartment. The old woman stared up at her. Se-oh had been told that complications from diabetes had rendered the woman's legs useless and kept her confined at home.

"Where's Jae-hyung?"

The woman craned to see behind Se-oh. She looked like she would refuse to let Se-oh enter until Jae-hyung arrived. Jae-hyung had gotten into an accident while delivering groceries and had to wear a cast for four weeks. If not for that stroke of luck, it would have been much, much longer before Se-oh came to #101. In fact, she might never have come. Jae-hyung handled all of their elderly customers. Even Wu-sul found them overwhelming.

"Jae-hyung is busy."

"How busy could he be that he can't even stop by? A store that small couldn't possibly have that many customers. Don't think I don't know he and the boss just sit around goofing off and chatting all day. Did something happen to Jae-hyung? He should have at least called to tell me he couldn't make it. . . . Or if he really is busy, then he could come later. When did you start working there? I heard they were hiring. I guess you're the one employed there now? Ha, employed. Fancy word for a place no bigger than a booger. Not like you have to get all dressed up to work there."

Se-oh didn't say anything. Jae-hyung would have gotten down on his knees and made eye contact with the old woman as they spoke. Se-oh stood up straight, her face blank, and only looked down at the old woman when she absolutely had to. The old woman seemed to have tired of holding her head up, or maybe she'd realized that Se-oh was not the soft and warmhearted type like Jae-hyung, because she finally moved aside for Se-oh and said, "You can put the stuff down in there."

Se-oh took her first step inside. Her head was spinning. Everything was falling into place. It scared her, too, to think that something could happen right then and there. She trembled as she took off her shoes and stepped into the living room. She was certain that, at any moment, Su-ho would open one of the inner doors and appear before her.

She let out a long breath. She thought she'd be too nervous to breathe normally, but she was okay. The further inside she went, the less sunlight reached her. She felt like she was crawling deep into the earth. The strange smell and trapped heat didn't help. The apartment didn't seem to get any ventilation. The windows were so firmly closed they looked like they'd never been opened at all.

The fishy, muddy smell and the relentless heat and humidity seemed to be coming from the enormous pot boiling in the kitchen. Blue flames rising from a portable gas burner on a low table licked menacingly at the sides of the pot. It looked like it had been sitting there boiling away in the same spot for years.

Se-oh took a quick look around at the apartment overtaken by thick, fishy air. Two rooms. Kitchen in disarray. A tiny, ancient television set sitting directly on the floor. A mirror, the frame caked with dust. Photos and colorful fake flowers on top of a side table. A long floor cushion that the old woman probably lay on.

The old woman paused in the middle of scooting across the floor to look up at Se-oh.

"Did Jae-hyung quit?"

"No."

"Then why didn't he come?"

"Where do you want this?"

"My goodness, you've got a temper. What's the big hurry?"

"These are the rough-skinned apples you ordered."

"Let me see."

The old woman took the apple that Se-oh handed her and slowly stroked it like she was stroking a child's face. She did the same with all five apples. The palms of her hands looked rougher than the apple skins.

"I can't use these."

She rolled four of the five apples back to Se-oh.

"How dare you bring me rotten apples. My legs may be useless, but my hands and eyes still work fine. I can tell those have no flavor. I don't have to taste them to know. I may as well eat a radish instead."

She sounded bent on seizing this opportunity to nitpick.

"And look at these green onions. The ends are all yellowed. How am I supposed to make warm salads with these? It'd just be a waste of dressing. And the cucumbers. They're no bigger than seeds. Can't even fit a knife in there."

Se-oh put the items the old woman rejected back into the basket. She'd been told that anything that wasn't perfect or that displeased the old woman in even the slightest way had to be taken back and exchanged, including the packaged foods with expiration dates that were coming up too soon. Jae-hyung had warned Se-oh about her, but she had just figured the old woman was pickier than other customers.

But it wasn't so much that the old woman was simply cranky. Bored from spending her days alone, she did what she had to do to find herself someone to talk to. Complaining about items from the store meant a chance to talk. And sending items back and placing multiple orders meant more opportunities to talk.

Wu-sul had told Se-oh to do whatever the old woman asked. The woman's son had made a point of asking them very earnestly to be patient with his mother, and Wu-sul felt sorry for her, as the once-active woman who'd enjoyed poking her nose into everyone's business was now confined to her home.

"Finding the right person for the job is everything. But where'd they find you? What a shame. Can't believe they'd hire such a sullen brat."

Se-oh knew the old woman was only trying to get her attention, but she pretended not to notice and asked, "Mind if I get a glass of water?" The woman scowled and gestured toward the kitchen.

From the pot on the gas burner came the awful smell of a once-living thing put through a long boil. Jae-hyung had told her it was simmered eel. Se-oh held her breath as she looked around the kitchen.

And then she found it. Brown, and stretched out long and thin like a snake. No bigger around than her thumb but as malignant as a viper. Se-oh stared, possessed, at where it clung to the wall. Worn-out and soft with age. Black with years of accumulated grease. Capable of sparking a tremendous blaze. It could happen now if she wanted it to. What had happened at #157. What had happened to her father. To Se-oh. And now, soon, to Su-ho.

"What's the matter? Can't find the water?" the old woman called out impatiently. Se-oh took her time filling a glass.

"Hang on," the old woman said. "Take this to Mr. Kim."

She turned off the gas burner and opened the pot lid. Steam filled the room. Se-oh couldn't stop herself from gagging. The old woman clucked her tongue at Se-oh and filled a plastic container with hot broth.

"Stop making that face. This is health food. For my son. I always send some to Mr. Kim, too."

The woman wrapped the container in a square of cloth and handed it to Se-oh.

As Se-oh was slipping her shoes back on, the old woman grabbed her ankle. Se-oh jumped. The old woman smirked and released her hand.

"You got nice, thick ankles. Bring me a daikon radish that looks just like them tomorrow. I'm going to slice it up and make a salad. I've been in the mood for radish lately."

Her voice was soft, but the look on her face was hard. Though it could have been the fault of the darkness.

"You'll suffer when you're old."

"Excuse me?" Se-oh asked.

Muttered under her breath, the old woman's words sounded like she was casting a spell.

"When you get old, whatever you used in your youth is the first to go. Arms, legs, eyes—they all have an expiration date. When I was young, there was nowhere I didn't go, and now look at my legs. I ran all over this city, selling my wares. . . . All the way to Hawolgok-dong, Uijeongbu, Mullae-dong, Cheolsan-dong,

Sangwangsimni-dong, Myeonmok-dong . . . I'd put my basket on my head and take off for another place, put it down, hoist it back onto my head, and run off again."

The old woman's muttering went on and on. Se-oh understood bits and pieces of it. Luckily, it wasn't a prophecy, foretelling Se-oh's bleak future. The old woman was merely bemoaning her own bad luck.

But no matter how she tried to put it out of her mind, the old woman's words sounded like they were meant for her. If you don't mend your ways, your legs will fail, your arms will lock, you'll drool each time you speak, food will spill down your shirt when you try to eat, you'll mutter the same unintelligible thing over and over, and in the end you won't remember who you are. . . . If what the old woman had said was true, then Se-oh's heart would be the first to go. Because it had harbored malice, fostered hatred, and lived with sadness without a moment's rest.

The old woman sat on the cold floor and talked and talked. Just to keep from being alone. Se-oh stared down at the woman, the smell from the plastic container filling her nose. She continued standing, silent and expressionless, until the old woman finally realized that Se-oh was simply waiting for her to stop talking.

22

Lying in the goshiwon bed, Se-oh pictured the moment when her father, having finished his preparations, must have sat on the couch and stroked the lighter. What went through his mind when he smelled the gas? Did he look around at the house to bid it farewell? Did he open the door to Se-oh's room one last time before flicking the lighter? Did he take a final look at the framed photo on top of the credenza, the one of baby Se-oh and her young mother? She couldn't stop picturing him then, after those moments had passed and it was time for him to sit back down on the sofa, staring around at the house in a daze, unable to make up his mind. It pained her that all she could do was try to imagine it, that she would never know for sure what really happened.

She had known, however vaguely, that something was weighing on her father. Every single day, someone had come to visit him, and her father had waited outside in the courtyard to keep that person from coming into the house, or had sent Se-oh away on errands to prevent her from running into him, though now and then the person's voice had wormed its way through the closed front door anyway. And yet, Se-oh had never once asked her father what was wrong. She never even wondered who this person was who kept visiting. The voice through the door was sharp and angry, but she never bothered to think about who it might belong to. As if, the moment she started to care, she would lose the protection that she so needed from her father. Even when he sent her to go pick up the coat, she'd casually dismissed it as an unexpected birthday gift. She thought she was simply receiving something that was owed her.

It had taken Se-oh this long to understand why her father had sent her out on errands all the time. Back then, she'd assumed he was getting fed up with her never leaving the house. But now she realized those were probably the days when he had to suffer great humiliation at the hands of Su-ho. The days when he couldn't pay what he owed, or when he had to push the due date back. Days when he had to grovel and beg.

She often tried to recall whether he'd hesitated before sending her out, and whether he'd tried to bring himself to say something. Even if he had acted differently than usual, she would have been too lazy to question it. She blamed herself. Why hadn't she tried to make him feel better? Why was she so far away when her father was simultaneously wishing for death and hoping for rescue? Why did she never once ask her father anything? Why did she leave him on his own to suffer like that? Why did she allow him to see himself as incompetent and powerless and to become so convinced he was hurting his daughter's future that he ended up mistaking the worst possible decision for the lesser of two evils?

She had been completely indifferent to her father when they were together. She was so busy seething about having spent several years of her precious twenties locked up in a tiny room, raging at the death trap Mi-yeon had dragged her into, and picturing in fear the resentment of those she'd dragged down with her, that she had no energy left to spare for her poor father.

Every time those thoughts haunted her, she grabbed the hammer. She wasn't really aiming it at Su-ho. She was aiming it at herself for doing nothing but brooding over her own misfortune, for not paying any attention to anything around her because she was too busy wallowing in her own regret, and for ignoring her father's loneliness and suffering. But she never brought the hammer down. She lacked the courage.

After leaving #101 with the smelly plastic container, the stench would not leave her hands. Even after handing it off to Wu-sul and washing her hands several times, then returning to the goshiwon and washing her hands several more times, the smell remained. The old lady had said she made that concoction for her son three or four times a month. The days she placed the pot on the burner, the smell would be especially foul. At last Se-oh had found a way to put her plan into action. The ever-present stench. It turned out there were days when it was even stronger. The smell would assist her.

If her goal was simply to inflict harm, then there were other ways to go about it. She could consider outsourcing. All she had to do was save up a lot of money. Then she could hire a talented and experienced hitman to arrange a car accident or toss him off a building. But the important thing wasn't Su-ho's death. What mattered was that Se-oh would be the one delivering the blow.

The intent to murder had no defense. Even if it did, it was still wiser to turn to the law than to pursue justice on your own. The law was a mechanism put in place to prevent people from doing so. Se-oh, too, could appeal to the law if she wanted to. Aiding and abetting suicide was enough to be taken in for questioning. If convicted, Su-ho would face anywhere from one to ten years in prison. But how was she to explain how he caused it to happen? There was no point in even trying. The law could not relieve her of the suffocating oppression she felt. It wouldn't even so much as lend her an ear. It wasn't the law's job to do so.

The real problem was that Su-ho was *technically* innocent. Sure, he would have resorted to verbal abuse in the process of demanding payments. He would have called nonstop, dropped in unannounced, and disrupted her father's daily routine. He would have overstepped his legal bounds. But there was no way to prove any of that.

The only people harmed by Se-oh's father's death were Se-oh and her father. Se-oh knew this. Su-ho's death would not change any absurd laws, and it would not bring her father back. It would do nothing to lift the spirits of those like her father whose self-esteem had been damaged by debt.

And yet, by intending to see it through, by willingly fostering malice and contemplating and picturing murder, she was able to go on living even after losing everything. She would not have been able to get through the hours if she did not have a purpose. Everything had gone up in flames with #157. Including Se-oh. She was so convinced of it that she felt puzzled when other people looked at her or talked to her or tried to make her smile. Each time, instead of feeling the simple pleasure of being alive, she thought about how to put her plan into action. She obsessed over which method she would use, how she would make it possible, when she would do it, whether it was better to reveal her identity to Su-ho or keep him in the dark to the end, and what she would say to him if they were face to face.

The thought of Su-ho dying did nothing to alleviate Se-oh's

suffering. She knew the identity of the pain that gripped her insides. The truth was that it had nothing to do with Su-ho.

It was awful to sustain a life on thoughts of killing someone. Malice kept Se-oh alive, but it did not let her live. It fed her, but it also turned her stomach and made her throw up. It enabled her to bear the hours spent lying in the goshiwon, but it also gave her nightmares. It helped her to live among others, but each time she saw other people, she fantasized about death and felt guilty. She was skeptical. If all she could think about was murder, if that was what filled her head day in and day out, then what was to become of her in the future?

She decided that she would find herself another life later. Though, once it was all over, she would probably ask herself why she'd been so obsessed with this. She might even be so consumed by the question that she wouldn't have any energy to spare to look for another life. In fact, when she thought about it, maybe a new life wasn't something you were allowed to have anyway.

She could hear a television playing somewhere. On nights like this, she got no sleep at all. That background murmur was like someone whispering in her ear; her fear of it raised the hairs on the back of her neck. No matter how she tried to sleep, the muffled noise from the karaoke rooms downstairs never failed to wake her. The constant thumping bass sounded like someone rapping and rapping at a thin door.

Se-oh stared up at the bottom of the cupboard mounted above the bed, and tried to put everything that had happened to her father in order. At first her thoughts were just a jumble of sentences. She strung the related sentences together. As she did so, she invariably discovered holes, mistakes, and misunderstandings hidden among them. For example, lines like "Dad is hounded by debt collectors" and "The house isn't enough for collateral" managed to connect with "Dad chooses suicide." But "Dad chooses suicide" and "Se-oh is left alone" refused to connect no matter what. She had to figure out all of the missing lines between them. Some would never be found.

She got up, sat on the edge of the low, creaky bed, and took the items out of the cardboard box she'd brought with her from #157. She stood the porcelain figurine on the desk, slipped her feet into her father's shoes, and put on the half-burned glasses. Then she clomped back and forth across the tiny room in the too-big shoes, the glasses distorting the size and texture of everything. The person in the next room banged on the wall to tell her to keep the noise down.

As she reached into the box for the bundle of letters wrapped in twine, a strange feeling came over Se-oh. Nothing was missing from the box. The problem was that everything was slightly different. She had always put the stack of letters back in with the knot facing down, but this time it was facing up.

She tried to chalk it up to her mood. She wasn't the type to set trivial rules and then actually remember them and stick to them day after day. It was simply a fleeting sense of unfamiliarity, a feeling brought on by the fact that everything in the box now seemed to have been ruthlessly organized. Se-oh normally grabbed items spontaneously and put them back at random, but the items in the box had been placed there in a deliberate and orderly fashion. The idea that someone else might have touched the box left Se-oh feeling unsettled.

Of course, she might have only been feeling that way because of the notice posted in the goshiwon entrance. It stated that an occupant's face lotion that they'd used just the night before was gone when they woke in the morning. In other words, someone had opened their door and stolen it while they were sleeping. The only people who would've been surprised by that were those who were brand-new to goshiwons. With time, goshiwon residents stopped being surprised when their toothpaste or slippers or toiletries got swiped.

Just to be sure, Se-oh opened the desk drawer and cabinet. Nothing else was amiss. There was no sign that anyone had rifled through the contents and taken anything. Not that there was anything worth taking.

She tried the doorknob anyway. It was locked. When she'd first moved in, she had frequently forgotten to lock the door. She kept thinking of it as just a room, not as a home. Every morning she would wake and open the door only to shock herself at the fact that she'd slept all night with it unlocked. She didn't do that anymore. Enough time had passed for her to get it through her head that it was not a room, it was her home now. She had also, when she first moved in, done her best to walk as quietly as possible down the hallway so as not to disturb anyone. After getting hit a few times by doors opening suddenly, she'd acclimated to the goshiwon life enough to know that it was better to make noise.

Se-oh stared hard at the doorknob and did not move. As if there were someone standing on the other side.

23

As the express bus to J— passed through the tollgate, Ki-jeong stared out the window, her back stiff. Thinking about what had happened to her sister there revived the low thrum of horror she'd been feeling ever since that first call from the police.

She'd made her way to J— by retracing her sister's steps, beginning with the phone records the police had given her. She had fixated on Se-oh's phone number and ignored the other numbers. All because she'd accepted her sister's suicide as so much a matter-of-course that she didn't even question it.

The phone records were sparse. Especially for a month's worth of calls. Other than spam and telemarketers, most of the days had passed without a single call. When a call was made, it lasted less than a minute. All of the calls with Ki-jeong had ended very quickly. There was one record of a call around 8:00 p.m. that had lasted just over a minute. That was the longest.

Ki-jeong had probably finished dinner and sat down to watch a TV show with her mother. She usually dealt with her after-work stress by staring at the TV or eating. When her sister called, she would have gotten up and slipped into the other room to answer it. Her mother would have glanced over but pretended not to notice. She would have known who was calling. What would they have talked about in under a minute? She couldn't remember. First, the standard greetings: How've you been? Good, you? Next: How's teaching? Okay, how's college? All the usual questions.

Her sister would have done the talking while Ki-jeong listened. That was how it went. After saying hello, Ki-jeong would wonder what to say next and, coming up with nothing, she would sit in silence until her sister started talking about things like the people she'd met in her latest student group or how she'd begun studying for the TOEIC exam again. Looking back on it now, her sister's stories were all the same. It was always something about some new endeavor that wasn't going as she'd hoped, or about how much she depended on her fellow group members.

As for the other calls, she'd been able to guess what had happened by the time stamps. Ki-jeong never took her sister's calls when she was with other people. It was too much trouble to explain about her sister. Each time, she would answer just long enough to say, "I'll call you later," and then hang up. Sometimes she did call later, but most of the time she didn't. Their last phone call had probably been the same. The last words Ki-jeong probably heard from her were, "Sorry, Sis." That was what she said every time to her busy older sister.

Other than spam, telemarketers, Se-oh, and Ki-jeong, there were only three phone numbers left. When she'd dialed the first one, a man answered. He sounded rushed. She told him her sister's name, but he said he didn't know her. Ki-jeong explained briefly why she was having to call him out of the blue to ask who he was. He didn't seem too surprised.

"I'm a deliveryman."

"May I ask where you normally make deliveries?"

"Sillim-dong."

Sillim-dong was the neighborhood in Seoul where her sister had lived. Ki-jeong let out a breath. The more she found out about her sister, the less she seemed to know her. She grew more distant as things grew more certain.

"If I come to the office, would I be able to see the delivery slip or find out what was delivered that day?"

"You can if you want, but it won't be worth the trip."

"Excuse me?"

"It would've been a book. I make deliveries for an online bookstore."

Three days before she'd died, her sister had bought a book and planned to read it. Did suicidal people order books? Of course, Ki-jeong knew that some deaths came on impulse. She knew, too, that her sister didn't lack the tendency. She saw her sister's life as one of drifting from one unforeseen crisis to another without anywhere to anchor her heart. That was why she had been so quick to assume her sister's death was a suicide.

But it was still far-fetched to assume that someone who'd shown no signs of suddenly tying up loose ends, someone who'd bought a book presumably with the intention of reading it, would choose death by drowning, and in J— of all places, where they had basically no connections.

Ki-jeong had kept asking herself questions she couldn't possibly answer. As these unanswerable questions continued to pile up, she found herself abruptly questioning her sister's death, which she'd regarded as settled.

Why had she been so quick to conclude, upon seeing her sister's corpse, that this was a long time coming? She hadn't even requested an investigation, so certain was she that her sister had committed suicide. She never even considered the other possibilities. Which was not to say that she thought someone had pushed her sister into the river to her death. That thought was more frightening than imagining her sister had jumped on her own. But it could have been an accident. Maybe, rather than drowning herself because she couldn't overcome her despair, she'd simply slipped. An unintended mishap.

A woman had answered at the second phone number. She sounded relaxed, sleepy. She did not recognize Ki-jeong's sister's name at first. When Ki-jeong briefly explained, she said she didn't know her but then double-checked and said, Aha, #216. It was the owner of the goshiwon where her sister had stayed. The woman said she had probably called Ki-jeong's sister to try to collect on late rent. And that that was the only reason she would ever call a tenant directly.

When Ki-jeong told the goshiwon's building manager her sister's name, he handed her a cardboard box that had been tucked to one side in the storeroom. He said he'd collected the items from her room while getting it ready for the next tenant. The box contained a few pieces of clothing and several test prep books for the civil service exam. It also held a can of soda, some toiletries, and a partnerless slipper. And one book, in pristine condition. A Philip Roth novel.

Had this stuff really belonged to her sister? The only thing that had her name on it were the test prep books. The rest of it could have belonged to someone else, and Ki-jeong would have been none the wiser.

The manager would not let her into #216. It was occupied. They couldn't keep an unpaid room empty for long. Ki-jeong stood in front of the door to #216, where her sister had lived for several months. The doors were so closely spaced together that she couldn't believe how small the rooms must be.

The dark, cramped room would have a chair with a wonky leg. The desk organizer would contain a bottle of Tylenol, and the blankets would be in the same constant state of disarray. Inside the cabinet would be extra-spicy instant noodles, the smallest size container of microwavable rice, and a can of hot pepper–flavored tuna. Perhaps her sister, too, had had only a single electric blanket to get her through cold nights in the goshiwon. It was easy for Ki-jeong to picture the inside of #216. She simply pictured the inside of #433, Se-oh's room.

Ki-jeong felt guilty that she'd taken an interest in her sister only after her final moments had come and gone. She'd never really known her. And now here she was, imitating a detective just so she could quell her guilty conscience. She didn't have to look any further than herself to find someone who'd neglected her sister. She despised herself for it. Maybe that's what Ki-jeong's sister had wanted her to feel and why she'd continued to send her to Se-oh's cramped goshiwon or off in search of this Bu-wi person.

Her sister's life had been colored by her mother and father's lives, and the lives of all the people she'd known or loved. By ending that life, her sister had made a choice, or perhaps had refused to make any further choices. Which was why Ki-jeong needed to find these two people who shared a final connection with her sister.

Her only recourse was Se-oh. She had contacted the private investigation firm again. The person on the other end was cheerful, unlike Ki-jeong, who tripped over her own tongue and took forever to say why she was calling. When Ki-jeong had hesitated, worrying over legal issues and what would happen if she was found out, the person reassured her that entering a goshiwon was not even on the spectrum of criminal activities. They'd added that a single piece of wire was all she would need for that type of door. Ki-jeong had made up her mind as gravely as if she were agreeing to do a favor for someone else.

She broke into Se-oh's room twice. It was like an oversized shoebox. A room that had been built purely for economy, without any space for rest or secrets. A room that was little more than a bed in a partitioned hallway. Like all things manufactured for simple efficiency, the slightest glimpse inside released an astonishing reek of poverty. The windowless room felt mercilessly isolated. The noise from neighboring rooms came through loud and clear.

The trench coat. It was the first thing that caught her eye when she stepped into the darkened room. She couldn't tell it was purple until she turned on the light. The more she looked at it, the more strangely touching it seemed. Not because it sagged there like a person hanging by their throat. But because the color and design were so completely out of place in that room.

Se-oh never fixed her bed but simply left the blankets in the same spot as when she rose in the morning. Her O's were shaped more like teardrops than circles. Judging by the size of her pants, she weighed a lot more than Ki-jeong. The items in the box were all jumbled together, suggesting that she went through it frequently. And judging from the burn marks, Ki-jeong guessed that the items had been salvaged from Se-oh's house.

Being in the room told Ki-jeong how unfair it was to question Se-oh about her sister's death. Se-oh was just a girl in her mid-twenties who'd lost her home in a fire and was now living in a goshiwon. Considering how many of the sentences scribbled in her notebook were about missing her father, Ki-jeong figured that she'd lost her father in the same fire. And she inferred from the fact that Se-oh wrote a lot more about her father that she must have lost her mother or been separated from her a long time ago. It wasn't that she didn't miss her mother. She just missed her a little less.

As a child, Se-oh would never have imagined this future for herself. She would never have guessed that she would lose her parents early, and that the best years of her life would be spent in a room hardly bigger than a coffin.

That thought made Ki-jeong want to straighten out the rumpled bed sheets and make the bed up neatly, fold a thick piece of paper and stick it beneath the wonky chair leg to balance it, attach a deadbolt to the flimsy goshiwon door, and take the purple trench coat off of the dingy wall, place it in a clean garment bag, and hang it in a closet.

While she was in the room, she read the notebook in the cabinet and the letters in the box, selecting them at random. The letters were old and from a girl named Mi-yeon Cho. They were mostly filled with her trying to prove she was a good friend. It was common for kids that age to force friendship on others.

Some of the lines written in the notebook were hard to overlook. Completely indeterminate sentences, such as "Not yet." Short, abrupt greetings, such as "Goodbye, Dad." Commonplace resolutions, like "Absolutely no mistakes." And harder words with no context to aid understanding, like "hose cock."

The more she read, the clearer it was that the contents of the notebook concerned Se-oh and Se-oh only. They had nothing whatsoever to do with her sister. Given the lack of a clear subject, most of it was impossible to follow. Either there was too little information or too much, making it useless for her. But there was one thing that caught her interest. The ongoing list of someone's whereabouts. Even at a glance, it looked like several months' worth.

The entries included specific times:

8:43 Station, convenience store
Lunch, octopus soup restaurant
17:45 Gojan 138-2
19:07 Rail station, Yangpyeong blood sausage soup
20:46 Office
22:13 Station
22:58 Through the construction site
23:04 Arrival

At first she thought it was Se-oh's schedule. Though it was a slightly strange way to organize a daily itinerary. But she soon realized it wasn't. No one would ever organize their day that way. Se-oh had been tracking someone who'd arrived at the subway station near work around eight forty-five in the morning, worked in Gojan-dong in the afternoon, and returned to the office where they'd stayed until ten o'clock at night.

Who was this Se-oh person following, and why? Since Ki-jeong herself had been reduced to sneaking into someone else's room, she understood that Se-oh did not necessarily have some criminal intent or particularly strange predilections.

The express bus arrived at the final stop. While the other passengers disembarked, Ki-jeong sat stock still. It all felt so distant, the things that had happened here, the facts that would soon be uncovered. The driver gestured for Ki-jeong to hurry up. Ki-jeong slowly took her first step into J——.

She caught a taxi outside the station. The wind didn't feel as cold as it had in Seoul. Ki-jeong had come over three hundred kilometers, nearly from one end of the country to the other. She was on the other side now, as if the distance traveled were a measure of the time that had passed since viewing her sister's corpse. Meanwhile, she had learned the names Se-oh Yun and Bu-wi. She had been to the goshiwon where her sister lived and snuck into Se-oh's room. And yet her sister was still a mystery. The more she learned, the deeper and darker the hole went.

But now, maybe, she would be able to fill in that hole a little bit. The third person she'd called would tell her something. Maybe she would also learn more about Se-oh. Ki-jeong got out of the taxi and headed for that person.

24

Watching the tenement flats at night on the weekend was like listening to midnight radio. Lots of quiet sounds that did not rattle the nerves. Lights turning on in one window and off in another like songs changing.

She heard movement near the entrance. Se-oh hid behind a corner of the debris netting that surrounded the place like a brick wall. It was especially dark there, as the glow from the streetlights did not reach. The sky was even darker. The air was so cold that the moon looked frozen. The footsteps passing the building grew fainter.

There were three or four households that hadn't moved out yet. Lights flickered like distress signals in several of the windows, and every now and then she could hear the sounds of a television playing or a child crying.

The lights were out in Su-ho's apartment. If she stared hard, she could just make out the colorful glow of a television through the window. That meant Su-ho wasn't home yet. The old woman never turned on the living room light until he was. His apartment looked like a black wall. Which might have been why Se-oh found herself thinking about the pyramid's dormitory.

By day, all she could think of was escaping, and yet by night she had flocked back with everyone else. Being with others enabled her to return. Though once she was inside and surrounded by other people, she could barely stand it.

The window in the dorm room had always been closed. It wasn't left that way on purpose but had simply rusted shut with age. When they scrubbed the room from top to bottom once a month, they could crack it open a tiny bit with great effort. One day, while everyone was rushing around, busy cleaning, one girl had stood in front of the window doing nothing. It was the girl Bu-wi had brought in. She'd been holding out for several months without any success.

As she stared out through the crack in the window, others had asked her as they passed by, "What're you looking at?"

What they really meant was that she should get to work, but she didn't understand and innocently said, "The sky."

"You can see it?"

"Yes, the weather's very clear today," she'd responded cheerfully.

Bu-wi had stroked her hair lovingly, as if she were his little sister. Se-oh had watched her carefully, and after they were done cleaning, she'd gone to the window. The sky was not visible. A gray wall surrounding a construction site had blocked it from view.

The view was probably the same from Su-ho's apartment. Their veranda window no doubt looked directly onto the high debris netting. By the time it was taken down, the building would have been long demolished with not a trace left behind.

Se-oh had worked out the details of her plan one step at a time, like adding bricks to a wall. It had taken her a while, but now she was nearing the end. Her plan would soon be put into action. But it seemed like something unexpected might interfere at any moment. The thoroughness of her plan might unravel, or her resolution might weaken. It was impossible to know whether coincidence would interfere at the decisive moment. All she could do was try to anticipate what was coming and wait for it.

As she imagined her labor coming to fruition, she realized how callous she'd become. She felt no sadness, no guilt. She admitted this without sentiment. She felt no compassion for Su-ho or his aged mother, either. Nor for herself, clinging hopelessly to this plan of hers. If she felt any emotion connected to her plan, it was envy toward Su-ho for the world he was about to reach. The unfamiliar world called death.

A little after nine, she left the shadows of the darkened tenement flats. On the way to the station, she stopped at a phone booth and slowly dialed her old number. It rang for a long time. She imagined it ringing to no avail inside the ruins of #157. But, of course, that didn't happen. There was nothing left of #157.

Next she dialed another number. She'd pictured herself dialing it so many times in her head that she had it memorized. Someone answered on the third ring. Their wheezy voice traveled through the receiver. Se-oh said nothing. The other person breathed deliberately, like an animal sizing up its adversary, and then suddenly shouted.

"Who the hell are you? Why are you doing this to us?"

The old woman sounded terrified. She was breathing hard, her voice sharper and shriller than necessary. Se-oh didn't respond.

"Why are you doing this to my son?" the woman yelled again.

Some animals raise their quills when they're scared. Some change color. Some spit venom. The old woman screeched. She was still breathing hard. Se-oh couldn't make out any other sounds. If Su-ho had been home, he probably would have grabbed the phone from his mother and yelled for her.

"Please stop."

This time the old woman begged. Se-oh could practically feel her breaths through the phone. She did not hang up.

"When my son gets his hands on you, he's going to kill you!"

The pleading had not lasted long. With that last roar, she hung up.

Se-oh slowly put the phone back in its cradle. The fear in the old woman's voice had taught her something unexpected. Someone had threatened Su-ho before. More than once. And recently, it seemed.

25

The hallway was as dark as if it were pouring rain outside. But the cold did nothing to deter the smell of instant noodles and mold. People kept coming and going. Noise was coming from every direction—from inside the rooms, from people chatting in the common area, from the speakers thumping downstairs in the karaoke bar. Shards of light reached out from beneath the room doors like pieces of broken china and gave off no warmth. The door to #433 was dark.

Ki-jeong had been drawn back to this place after meeting Bu-wi. When she had made that third phone call, she'd let the phone ring for a long time before a man finally answered. He'd sounded very happy to hear her sister's name. That was a first. To come across someone who not only recognized her sister's name right away but was excited to hear it. She had wondered whether the phone number would turn out to be Bu-wi's, and sure enough it was. His happiness quickly turned to suspicion. A normal reaction for someone receiving an unexpected call from a friend's family member.

When she met Bu-wi in J—, he'd talked nonstop about her

sister. He told her everything he knew. Or at least, she had the feeling he did. And yet the circumstances of her sister's death remained stubbornly unclear, to her dismay.

It would probably be the same after she met Se-oh. Se-oh would probably have very little, if anything at all, to tell her about her sister. Not because she had something to hide, but because there was nothing to tell. Nevertheless, she knew that Se-oh wouldn't go about her merry way, pretending not to know Ki-jeong's sister. As with Ki-jeong's sister, there was nothing merry or warm about Se-oh's life. She didn't exactly exude a youthful glow.

In talking to Bu-wi, Ki-jeong learned that her assumptions about the three of them—Se-oh, Bu-wi, and her little sister—were mostly wrong. They had each traveled along their separate, solitary paths, and at some point those paths crossed, and nothing more. Same as with everyone else. No one's lives were intimately bound together, but no one was entirely alone and unconnected either.

There was one thing she wondered about. All three of them had experienced similar failures. Time did not stop for them while they worked for the pyramid. They would have lost friends and time and hope. And money, too, of course. Bu-wi and Se-oh had probably taken out sizeable loans, just like her sister. But after experiencing identical failures, Ki-jeong's sister had died while Se-oh and Bu-wi survived. They'd survived, even if all that meant was that one of them was now tailing and keeping notes on someone, while the other was struggling to finish school on part-time wages in some podunk town. For some, despair brought an end to life; how was it that, for others, despair could bring about a new beginning, or just more of the same? What had caused her sister to fail at surviving and Se-oh and Bu-wi to succeed?

Though she could not know everything, there was one thing Ki-jeong could do. She could finish whatever it was her sister was meaning to say to Se-oh. What made Ki-jeong decide to risk misunderstanding and confront Se-oh was #433. The tiny, cramped goshiwon room with its paper-thin walls. The box of relics from #157 that Se-oh went through every day. It was because of the cheap bottles of toner and moisturizer; the previous day's hand-washed laundry, half-dry and stiff, hanging on coat hangers and on the back of the chair; the plain, white cotton underwear; the purple trench coat hanging permanently on the wall like a decoration. As Se-oh sat surrounded by these things, just as her sister had in #216, Ki-jeong wanted to tell her that someone still missed her.

A large group of people, chattering loudly, came out of the common area. Ki-jeong knew Se-oh would not be among them. They each went into their separate rooms, leaving Ki-jeong alone in the cold once more.

Someone was coming toward her. The person hadn't made a sound when they'd entered the building, and for a moment it was as if they'd suddenly materialized in the hallway. The yellowish light was too faint for Ki-jeong to make out the face, but she could see the hair was tied in a ponytail that swayed behind them, and the shoulders sagged. The silhouette looked like an old woman.

Ki-jeong stepped aside to let her pass. The person stopped in front of #433. She seemed conscious of Ki-jeong standing nearby as she cautiously took her keys out of her bag and unlocked the door. Ki-jeong watched from behind. The person was shorter than Ki-jeong had imagined. She was big-framed but not fat or sluggish. Instead, she gave off an impression of frailness.

Se-oh opened the door just slightly and stuffed herself inside.

The sound of locking echoed loudly down the hallway. The light leaking through the crack in the door reached Ki-jeong's feet. The warmth of the light surprised her.

26

If you run into someone you know, the doors to hell will reopen. That was what Se-oh had told herself when she was hiding out at home. That everyone always had it out for someone. She was convinced that the people she'd talked into joining her downline only to return home in failure, and the people she'd gotten into scuffles with when they'd stormed their way into the dorm and tried to drag her recruits back home with them—not that she had any idea why she'd bothered to fight them—would appear out of nowhere to scream and rage at her. Because hatred never went away, it only multiplied.

By sending her out of the house on regular errands, her father had shown her that the odds were high she would never see any of those people again. Look, he seemed to say. No one is out to get you. Everyone is just living their own life.

It had taken Se-oh forever to get it through her head. No one was paying that kind of attention to her. They were so busy making up for lost time and getting resettled that their hatred and resentment naturally wilted. Those emotions were useless in the face of daily life. Time overcame everything. She didn't even

resent Mi-yeon anymore. Which wasn't to say she no longer
cared. The fact that her name still haunted her was proof.

And so, she had continued to anticipate the moment someone
would come up to her and say, "Excuse me, but are you Se-oh
Yun?" The world was big, but coincidence was forever sending
people into each other's paths. She had imagined it so many times,
and yet she'd never once pictured it happening in the dark, narrow hallway of the goshiwon. There was no way this was coincidence's doing, though. To have it happen here meant this person
already knew nearly everything there was to know about her.

The woman she'd passed in the hallway knocked on her door
and said, "You must be Se-oh Yun."

Se-oh stared at her, but the woman's face was hidden in the
shadows. The person didn't live in the goshiwon. If so, she
would've said "hey" instead of calling Se-oh by name. Hey, have
you seen my other slipper? It looks like this. Hey, I think you used
my shampoo this morning. Hey, did you take the can of tuna I left
in the fridge? Hey, stop dragging your chair across the floor. It's
loud.

"I'm sorry for the sudden intrusion."

She didn't sound all that sorry. It was probably just something
the woman thought she had to say in order to get Se-oh to talk to
her. What did she look like? Se-oh had stared at the woman standing in the middle of the hallway like a pillar, had given her a look
that said get out of her way. She recalled slim pants and black flats.

Someone had finally found her. She had thought she would
feel scared and angry when this moment came, but she didn't.
Because she'd been imagining they would eventually track her
down and accost her, and because she'd wasted so much time try-

ing to avoid exactly that, now that it was really happening she wasn't as afraid as she'd thought she'd be.

How had this person found her? And who was she anyway? Was she one of the people Se-oh had slept shoulder-to-shoulder with all those years ago? Someone she'd shared a bathroom with, according to the time slots allotted them? Someone whose stench of sweat and excrement had become so familiar that they stopped feeling embarrassed or uncomfortable about how seldom they were able to bathe? Or was she one of the family members who'd come in person to rescue her latest recruit?

"I'm Ha-jeong Shin's sister."

Se-oh had never heard that name before.

"You knew Ha-jeong, right? I'm her older sister, Ki-jeong Shin."

The voice coming out of the darkness sounded brittle, like ice cracking. A look of fear flickered over the person's face, a look that said she might have the wrong person after all. The fact that Se-oh didn't recognize the name meant it was definitely someone she'd known during her days in the pyramid. She'd met so many people back then. She couldn't have put a face to the name, no matter how hard she tried. It wasn't that she'd forgotten. There were a lot of people living there at the time whose names she'd never learned. She couldn't even begin to count how many had left after just a day or two.

"Hey, could you go talk in the common area instead?"

The door to the room next to Se-oh's burst open just long enough for the occupant to bark at them in irritation. They couldn't see his face. Se-oh retreated into her room, as if the voice itself were pushing her back. Ki-jeong followed her, uninvited, and stood awkwardly just inside the door.

"You said your sister's name is Ha-jeong Shin?" Se-oh asked.

"Yes."

Ki-jeong sounded disappointed that Se-oh hadn't placed the name yet. Maybe she'd expected Se-oh to light up the moment she heard it. Or maybe she thought her face would crumble or flood with guilt.

Se-oh slowly closed the door. She felt calm. Maybe because the name Ha-jeong Shin didn't ring a bell.

"You don't remember her?" Ki-jeong asked.

Instead of answering, Se-oh sat on the edge of the cold bed. The room was so small that they'd have to sit down or else their faces would be nearly touching. She watched closely as Ki-jeong pulled out the chair and sat down without asking. The chair didn't tip. Ki-jeong seemed to know one of the legs was shorter than the others. In fact, ever since she'd first entered the room, she'd shown no surprise at how compact it was. Nor was she trying to sneak peeks around the room. Se-oh had thought at first that Ki-jeong was just being polite, but now she suspected otherwise. Ki-jeong had been in one of these rooms before.

They sat with their knees touching. Se-oh turned to the side to make a little more room. That was as far apart as the room would allow them to get. She'd had so many questions, but now not a single one came to mind. She wondered, too, why Ki-jeong wasn't speaking up first. Why had Ki-jeong come looking for her? How did she find her? Had she been in Se-oh's room before? The fact that she was the older sister of some person named Ha-jeong Shin, whom Se-oh had no memory of, told her nothing.

"I thought for sure you knew my sister," Ki-jeong said with a sigh. It was hard for her to get the words out. And what she had to say next would be even harder. She'd barely said anything yet, but already it seemed impossible to explain properly all that had happened with her sister.

"What about Bu-wi?" Ki-jeong asked. "Do you remember him?"

Se-oh raised her head and looked at Ki-jeong. It was the first time she'd heard his name from a stranger.

"He says he knows you well."

Se-oh said his name to herself, careful not to let any of the sounds escape her lips. She repeated it several times, and then there it was. A memory of Ha-jeong Shin. It had followed right on the tail of Bu-wi's name, as if they were linked. The girl who'd followed Bu-wi around like a lost puppy. That girl.

"Ha-jeong. I remember."

"Thank goodness."

Silence fell over the room. But it wasn't a stubborn and oppressive silence. It felt calm. The quiet reassured Se-oh. This visit from Ki-jeong might have nothing to do with what she'd been imagining. Ki-jeong hadn't come to criticize her about what she'd done in the past, or grab her by the collar and shout at her, or blame her for everything. After all, Ha-jeong had not been part of her downline. Bu-wi was the one who'd recruited her.

"I heard that you two lived in the same dorm."

"There were a lot of us living there." Se-oh realized that made her sound defensive. "I only went there to wash up and sleep. I was too tired to do anything else. Everyone kept to themselves. It wasn't like we were there on some weekend trip. We didn't choose to eat and sleep together because we were all friends."

It was her first time opening up to someone else about those days. It was easier than expected. The passage of time had nothing to do with it either. The person sitting across from her had no idea what it had been like or how it felt to sleep alongside so many strangers in a cramped room. She didn't know that going through something like that ate away at more than just your time.

Ki-jeong might have thought she knew something, but it wasn't as much as what Se-oh knew. If she really wanted, Se-oh could lie about what she'd done and how she'd lived while in that place. She could make it all up. Her lies and countless misdeeds needed no justification. But the thought of trying gave her no joy. It hadn't been anyone else's fault. As with everything else in life, she'd simply made a choice, suffered a loss, and failed.

"I thought maybe you and my sister were close."

Se-oh didn't respond.

"To be really honest, I didn't know my sister all that well," Ki-jeong added apologetically.

"I wasn't close with anyone there," Se-oh said. "It wasn't easy to make friends. Whenever someone new was brought in, all I thought about was how long they would last, how much they'd be worth. A lot of new recruits tried to run away their first night, so we'd chat them up about all kinds of stuff just to keep them from leaving. But I'd forget about them right away. It was impossible to become friends with someone who was always watching to keep you from escaping at night."

That was a lie. She'd trusted Bu-wi. Ki-jeong's sister probably had, too. And maybe Bu-wi had trusted someone in turn. Though they couldn't show it, everyone in that place had relied on someone else if they could. That said, Ha-jeong had never once turned to Se-oh. Se-oh wasn't the type people turned to.

Se-oh hesitated and then asked, "How is Ha-jeong doing now?"

The fact that it was Ha-jeong's sister who'd come to find her, and not Ha-jeong herself, finally weighed on her. There had to be a reason she wasn't hearing all of this from Ha-jeong directly.

"She's dead."

Ki-jeong hesitated and then added that Ha-jeong had drowned and that it wasn't clear whether it was an accident or suicide. She figured that would answer a few questions Se-oh might have. The look on Se-oh's face said she wasn't too surprised.

Ki-jeong slowly answered the rest of the questions that she guessed Se-oh wanted to ask. Such as how she'd tracked her down at the goshiwon, and why. She wasn't sure if the explanation was acceptable. Se-oh nodded now and then. Though the nods were probably just an unconscious reflex, Ki-jeong felt grateful for them anyway.

Se-oh was surprised. She'd had no idea Ha-jeong had tried calling her multiple times. Her father had never handed her the phone when it rang or told her who was calling. After she'd escaped from the dorm, the team leader and other team members had called relentlessly and even come to the house. Her father had known that she didn't want to talk to any of them. He would have hung up on Ha-jeong as well, or told her Se-oh wasn't home. Se-oh never answered the phone herself. When the doorbell rang, she did not open the door. If her father wasn't home, the phone would ring and ring until it stopped on its own, and if someone visited, they would go home with nothing to show for it.

"Why did she call me?"

Ha-jeong and Se-oh hadn't been close enough for phone calls. Se-oh felt like apologizing to Ki-jeong for that. Someone's last words had to mean something to the bereaved. The bereaved would sustain themselves on whatever meaning they managed to extract from those words, at least for a little while. But Se-oh had stolen Ki-jeong's opportunity to hear them. Maybe Ki-jeong had been brooding over it the same way that Se-oh had been brooding over her father's final moments.

"When did you see her last?" Ki-jeong asked instead of answering.

Se-oh thought about the verb tense of that question, about the difference between asking "When did you see her last?" versus "Have you seen her?" The latter continued into the present while the former belonged to the past. A question like that required time.

It was a long time ago. Back then. Back when she'd thought a single failure meant your whole life was over. When she'd tried so hard not to fail that all she did was fail, over and over. When she'd called strangers out of the blue to try to convince them to work for her, and begged and pleaded with friends to join her. When she'd taken turns with others just to be able to splash some water on her face over a utility sink. When the only words that came out of her mouth were a hypnotic chant about how you could succeed if you really tried. When she didn't leave, not because she thought she was going to make money, but because it was too hard to acknowledge that she'd messed up. When she'd been so good at saying things she didn't believe just to keep people she didn't care about from leaving.

Now she understood a few things about those days. Enough time had passed. The first was that maybe all of life was like that. Holding onto hope only to get bitten. Maybe it would happen to her again, and again.

Looking back on it now, it hadn't been so different from any other time. There'd been good, and there'd been bad. That was all. At the time, she'd thought all of it was bad. Because happiness had flitted on by while bad things had a way of lingering.

She thought maybe it wouldn't have been so bad if they had been given better things to sell or if they had been treated better. Bu-wi had said the system itself was unfair, as it had played to everyone's get-rich-quick fantasies. And in fact, Se-oh had decided at some point that the problem was structural, in order to soothe her own disappointment.

It had been so hard for her to leave, even though she'd known she wasn't getting anywhere with it. She thought if she could at least scrape by, then that would mean she wasn't failing. Thinking back on it now, even what she'd considered success had been pathetic. It was like a thin, iridescent film barely maintained by surface tension. As flimsy as it was, she'd fought so hard to hold onto it.

If Mi-yeon was the reason she'd joined, Bu-wi was the reason she left. Typical dependent, cowardly Se-oh. Right around the time that Bu-wi had been in the business for eight months, and Se-oh for a year and five months, Bu-wi slipped out of the room during a progress meeting. Se-oh followed stealthily. Bu-wi crossed the street during a break in the traffic. Se-oh hurried her steps. Any second now he'd be gone. She worried he would be put off by the convenience store cashier's inhospitality. And feared that he would be wounded by the police officer's indifference, would give in to his emotional injuries, would eagerly choose a path of self-torment.

She couldn't help feeling heartbroken, too, that Bu-wi seemed poised to leave without saying a word, just like Mi-yeon. She figured his cheerfulness, his laid-back attitude, his displays of enthusiasm, had all been an act to keep her reassured. Or maybe she was being too negative. She'd been through so much hardship already.

What she'd felt that day wasn't betrayal. It was pity. Bu-wi was someone she could depend on completely, but he'd only just turned twenty-two. He was barely a man, the last traces of boyhood having just left him. Se-oh imagined what would become of someone like him, who projected nothing but strength and resilience, once they were subjected to acute anguish. She feared Bu-wi would become exactly what she pictured.

She wanted to stop him. Just to hold on to the person who'd become her pillar. She did not want to stop him. Everyone else in that place was already half-dead. As was Se-oh. She didn't want to turn Bu-wi into the same. Both things were true. And that contradiction would make her stop him, despite feeling racked with guilt.

As Se-oh waited across the street, shuffling back and forth among pain and pity and anxiety, Bu-wi entered the convenience store. He did not hide. He looked around at the items for sale. He picked something up and put it down. He did not plead with the cashier for help or stare out the window looking hunted. After a moment, he stood at the counter in front of the window, where customers could snack on their purchases, and rested his chin in his hand. Then he began eating something. It looked like it could be a triangle kimbap. Or a small chocolate bun.

Four minutes passed. Se-oh decided to go back inside the training center. She did not want Bu-wi to know that she was secretly watching him. As she turned, she met the eyes of the team leader, who had been secretly watching her. She wasn't surprised to see her. The team leader didn't look surprised at being caught. They were all tangled up together. Just as Se-oh kept an eye on Bu-wi, the team leader kept an eye on Se-oh. If Mi-yeon hadn't left, it might have been her watching Se-oh instead. There'd been a time when the thought of being so tightly linked to other people had made it easier for Se-oh to bear living in such a cold, dark, lonely place. But she realized in that moment that she wouldn't be able to bear it much longer.

Later still, another thought would occur to her. The pyramid was little more than a pawnshop. With herself as collateral, she'd sold off every personal relationship she could. The more she worked, the more certain failure became. Whenever she told people the line of work she was in, they got angry at her, ordered her to stay away from them, and warned her to never call again. From the way they reacted, she may as well have been carrying an infectious disease.

No one in the pyramid was independent. They were all connected, above and below, in every direction. The more interconnected they were, the more they were praised for their independence. The people connected to you were your seed capital. Fickle seed capital that could blow away at any moment. Se-oh didn't hesitate to take advantage of whoever she had to, either. At the time, she didn't have the leisure to even question it. The only regret was having no one left to use.

Naturally, pawnshops did not return items in hock free of charge. A price had to be paid. And the price was always much higher than what you had received for the item. It was the same in the pyramid. Though she did not know it at the time, being promoted to ranks named after jewels, like diamond and sapphire, was not payment.

Bu-wi returned to the training center a short while later, breathing hard and smelling of something sweet and spicy. His parted lips looked full and dewy. His flushed cheeks gave off a boyish playfulness. Se-oh had known Bu-wi a long time. Despite what he thought, she'd never been in love with him. But in that moment, she truly adored him.

The people Se-oh had met in that business were the type who would never help others, not even a blind man they'd bumped into on the street. She doubted that Bu-wi would offer anyone help, either. Not that Se-oh had a preference for the kind and compassionate type. If anything, Bu-wi seemed more likely to tell a blind man to step aside and stop blocking his path.

People accustomed to acting as a group and living closely with others will suppress their true selves in order to comply with group decisions, but Bu-wi wasn't like that. He would have grown tired of the monotonous, flavorless meals and longed for something sweet. He would not have felt guilty about ditching everyone to eat alone; in fact, he would never have considered it a selfish act in the first place. He had probably gone by himself simply because he didn't have enough money to pay for anyone else's snacks.

Bu-wi had the innocence of someone who'd never been unfairly taken advantage of. Se-oh lacked that naivety. Which was good. Se-oh hated Mi-yeon, but Bu-wi would probably never think that he'd wasted his life because of Se-oh.

Bu-wi had turned to Se-oh, who was standing in the doorway and staring at him, and asked, "Were you waiting for me?"

"No."

"Then what are you doing?"

"Waiting to go to the bathroom."

Bu-wi glanced over at the bathroom door. The women's bathroom had only one stall and was always busy.

"Yeah, you look like you have to pee. Your face is turning yellow."

Se-oh smirked and then laughed out loud.

"I know a thing or two about making you laugh, don't I?" Bu-wi crowed, mistakenly thinking that Se-oh had been laughing at his joke.

But he was wrong. She hadn't been laughing at his joke. She would have laughed no matter what he'd said. He wasn't very tuned in to other people's moods and often missed social cues, but he would find out soon enough that he could make Se-oh laugh without any effort at all. Not that she was planning to tell him that. She liked having a secret.

Sharing was the rule there. Recruiting was done openly, reasons for success were explained, reasons for failure were analyzed in detail, case studies were examined, and strategies were plotted together. In the process, Se-oh forgot that they were all individuals with their own ideas and their own preferences. In fact, she was even forgetting to think about herself. Because they all shared one thought and moved with one purpose and will.

Bu-wi never complained about it, but he didn't exactly put up with it either. If he was hungry, he had no qualms about eating alone. He solicited glares by pointing out things he thought didn't make sense. He said there were better solutions to housing and feeding everyone and gave unwelcome suggestions, much to the irritation of everyone else, who'd put up with the hardships without complaining.

Se-oh kept a close eye on Bu-wi. She was so used to thinking of everyone as interconnected that she couldn't conceive of herself as an independent individual, but Bu-wi always put himself first. He knew what he liked, did what he wanted, and was intent on leading his life as he pleased.

Bu-wi had not asked her to go with him. He'd left first, and Se-oh had followed. *I'll help you leave.* He'd said those words to her once but had since forgotten.

Later, Bu-wi slipped out of the training center again. By then, he'd been doing it so often that Se-oh barely even looked up. Nor did the team leader, who kept an eye on Se-oh, or Ha-jeong, who secretly kept an eye on Bu-wi behind the team leader's back. Nevertheless, Se-oh went out to the stairwell to glance out the window and verify where he'd gone. Then she put on a friendly face, went back inside, and resumed spewing empty words to win the trust of the new recruits who'd arrived the day before to receive training.

After a while she saw Ha-jeong check the time. Se-oh spoke louder, laughed harder, and eyed Ha-jeong for her assistance. Ha-jeong hesitated a moment before bolting upright, her face stiff. Se-oh grabbed her arm. She could still remember the way it felt. Bone-thin and scaly with dried skin. "I'll go get him," Se-oh said. Ha-jeong nodded anxiously. She wouldn't have wanted Bu-wi to know that she'd been watching him.

Se-oh crossed the street. She didn't bother checking the convenience store. Bu-wi wouldn't be there. She knew. She'd seen him catching a taxi in front of the store. Right before the cab door closed, he'd glanced back at their building. Se-oh thought he'd spotted her in the window. She'd waited. For him to wave at her to join him. For him to smile and mouth the words, *Come on, let's go.* But Bu-wi did not. He'd left by himself. Without saying a word, just as Mi-yeon had done.

An empty cab pulled up. Before the door closed, she glanced back at the building, just as Bu-wi had done. This time she made eye contact with no one. Se-oh went straight home.

After returning home, she kept getting angry. While she had been trapped there—sleeping with too many strangers in a too-small room, eating food with zero nutritional value, washing dirty dishes in the bathroom because the kitchen was too tiny, washing her face over a utility sink, calling friends and people she barely knew to try to convince them to join her downline, falling deeper into debt; and failing over and over and over—all that time, the world had remained completely unchanged. The TV stations beamed out the same nonsense and drivel day after day. Students went to school and took their tests on schedule. Even her father, amid all his worry over his daughter, still slept in a warm home and landed a job as a shop assistant and went to work every day and earned a paycheck and chipped away at his interest payments. Just the thought of it all made Se-oh lose it.

When her anger finally subsided, it was replaced by worry. As if worry had been hiding right around the corner, waiting for that very moment. Only one thing worried her. She was afraid Bu-wi would wake up and realize that Se-oh was the reason for the time he'd lost. Sometimes she even found herself thinking she should go back to the pyramid and try harder, really make a go of it this time. That thought occurred to her every time she started thinking of herself as completely useless. Too scared to crawl back alone, she went searching for Bu-wi again.

Bu-wi had changed his home phone number, and there was no point in calling his cell since the team leader had confiscated everyone's. She worked up the courage to drop by the training center. It turned into quite the ordeal, but she was able to confirm that Bu-wi had not gone back. She went to his old church, but they told her he'd stopped coming a long time ago. Then she started loitering around his old college, hoping to run into him by pure chance. But wandering randomly around campus didn't help her to find out anything new. After targeting a few specific locations and lying through her teeth to multiple people, she learned the truth: Bu-wi had never really been a student there.

It made her feel better. Bu-wi wasn't hiding from her. She simply didn't know where to look. Which meant that she might still bump into him one day. When you're hoping for a coincidence, luck pretends not to see you, but when you don't want one, it extends a helping hand.

Just as she hoped she might bump into Bu-wi one day, she figured there was also a chance she could bump into Mi-yeon. Entirely by coincidence, of course. For all she knew, Mi-yeon might be out there searching for her, just as she was searching for Bu-wi. And if she was, Mi-yeon would find out that she had driven herself into a corner. She would know then that she'd been cut off from Se-oh completely. Just as Se-oh had learned the same through Bu-wi.

She didn't breathe a word of any of this to Ki-jeong. The only thing she could bring herself to comment on was Ha-jeong's skinny arms. Nevertheless, she found herself starting to talk. She told Ki-jeong that she couldn't remember the last time she'd seen Ha-jeong; that she'd figured she would never see Ha-jeong again; that Ha-jeong didn't have a knack for the business; that at first she'd seemed incompetent, but later it seemed she was simply bad at lying and had no interest in the work in the first place; that she looked like she was doing it against her will; that she seemed to feel guilty about having to lure her reluctant friends out with lies and beg and plead with them to join her; that she seemed like the quiet type and so they'd never opened up to each other, but Ha-jeong seemed genuine; that she was kind and friendly and popular with the others in the dorm; that she was optimistic and witty and made others laugh; that she was thoughtful enough to buy medicine for others when they weren't feeling well. . . .

As Ki-jeong listened, her head suddenly fell. She sobbed quietly. Se-oh wasn't sure why she was crying. Did she feel bad for what her sister had gone through? Was she sorry she hadn't taken better care of her while they were together? Or maybe she just missed her. It had been the same for Se-oh whenever she thought about her father. At first, she'd felt guilty for not having been there for him, but now she simply missed him.

Se-oh placed her hand on top of Ki-jeong's without thinking about it. It'd been so long since she'd initiated such a gesture that she felt awkward. She could feel every single quiver of Ki-jeong's hand. Ki-jeong began to weep loudly, like a child. After a moment, the person in the next room started banging on the wall. The sound startled Ki-jeong, and she stopped.

"I'm sorry. I'm causing trouble for you," Ki-jeong said, as she took a deep breath to calm herself. "I can't be sure, but I thought maybe Ha-jeong was trying to get hold of you to tell you something." She gave Se-oh a kind look. "Something about Bu-wi."

Se-oh faced her directly, hoping Ki-jeong would break the news to her slowly, to delay the moment when she would hear what had happened to Bu-wi.

Se-oh often despaired over the time she'd wasted. But all she could do was comfort herself with the thought that at least she'd left when she did. It was behind her now. She'd already forgotten so much of it. The people she'd met, the things she'd said, the places she'd stayed. It was easy. She willed herself to forget by pretending not to recognize people she knew and by lying whenever someone asked what she'd been doing with herself. What she didn't know was that memory could not be fabricated, sealed, or transformed that way.

While talking to Ki-jeong, she allowed herself to recall for the first time, calmly, the history she'd tried to conceal, the many types of failures, the names of those who'd suffered with her. It seemed Bu-wi remembered all of it. Or to put it more precisely, he hadn't tried to forget. Anyway, that was the impression she got from what Ki-jeong told her.

According to Bu-wi, the last time he'd seen Ha-jeong was when they happened to bump into each other at his new college. She was there to meet someone. He was sitting with friends in a small park behind the medical school when he saw Ha-jeong walking toward them.

Ki-jeong paused there. Bu-wi had said they met by chance, but it struck her in that moment that her sister had probably been looking for him. After quitting school, she'd kept going from place to place, and it hadn't seemed like she was simply traveling.

The thought didn't last long. Se-oh was staring at her like she was waiting to hear what was next. Ki-jeong decided to jump straight to explaining Bu-wi's personal circumstances. That seemed to be what Se-oh really wanted to hear anyway.

When Se-oh had met Bu-wi to recruit him, Bu-wi was homeless. He would have gladly agreed to any job offer, even if it had been a crab boat instead of a multi-level marketing scheme. As long as it came with room and board.

His troubles had begun during the summer vacation of his third year in high school. His father had expanded his business a couple of years earlier and overextended himself. The ensuing financial trouble was like a runaway train. Bu-wi knew there was no money for him to go to college, but he took the entrance exam anyway, and despaired to learn that he'd been accepted into the top medical school of his choice. If only his father's business had crumbled a year later, he'd thought pointlessly. He would have been in college already by then, and they could have figured something out. Or better still if he'd been ruined a year earlier. That would have bought them time to save up money for his tuition.

While he was working with Se-oh, word got out among the pyramid members that Bu-wi was a premed student at a prestigious private university in Seoul. Bu-wi hadn't told anyone. That was the doing of one of his high school friends, who'd stayed one night as a potential recruit and took off the next day. All of his high school friends had thought he was in college, and Bu-wi hadn't bothered to set them straight. It wasn't that he lied. He simply kept silent about what had happened to him and his family, and all of the things that had changed as a result.

The work did not go well. One by one, he called up everyone he knew. He trusted them, talked to them, and kept switching up his strategies, but it made no difference. He wanted to earn an astronomical amount of money that was possible in theory. A short-term part-time job wouldn't be enough to cover the tuition at that school and living expenses. He figured the others had failed because they'd resorted to lying and saying outlandish things in order to recruit new members. He thought if he just explained himself well enough and didn't force a choice on people, then he would do fine.

He did earn some money. Enough to buy a triangle kimbap. But it was absurd of him to think he could make enough to go to school and help his parents out. Every day he spent at the convenience store trying to satisfy his hunger, he realized this.

After leaving the pyramid, he spent the next two years focused solely on saving up money. He managed it through a combination of resourcefulness, patience, and stamina. After working the graveyard shifts in convenience stores, at gas stations, and on apartment construction sites, he made enough to reapply to medical school and was accepted to a school in J—, a town he'd never set foot in before.

Sometime after their chance meeting, Bu-wi saw Ha-jeong again. This time it was planned. They chatted briefly on a bench in the garden behind the medical school before Bu-wi had to rush off to his part-time job. Undeterred, Ha-jeong kept offering to make the long trip out to J— again, just to see him. Bu-wi had asked her how Se-oh was doing. The fact that he'd offered to help Se-oh pricked at his conscience.

Ha-jeong had remembered seeing Se-oh when she risked returning to the training center to find Bu-wi. Up until that point, she'd assumed that Se-oh and Bu-wi left together. Se-oh had asked Ha-jeong if she'd heard from him, and she'd answered, "Wasn't he with you?"

Bu-wi had told Ki-jeong he was shocked to hear that Se-oh had looked for him. He struck Ki-jeong as cheerful, strong-willed, and resourceful, but so busy worrying only about himself that he paid little attention to other people's feelings.

Bu-wi was further surprised to hear that Ki-jeong's sister had stayed for several more months after he left. He thought she was only working there because of him. Se-oh felt maybe she knew why Ha-jeong had stayed. It was probably for the same reasons she herself had stayed after Mi-yeon left.

Ki-jeong finished her long story and handed Se-oh a slip of paper with a phone number written on it. It was Bu-wi's. Se-oh took the note and traced the numbers as if to imprint them into her fingertips.

"Bu-wi was really shocked to hear that my sister killed herself.

He said it didn't make sense, and that they had plans to meet again in J— before the semester started. Obviously, my sister never showed. He also said she'd been studying for the civil service exam for a long time, and that she must have quit school and studied for the exam while working part-time. He said she probably didn't tell her loved ones because she felt bad about it."

Loved ones. The term felt so unfamiliar coming out of Ki-jeong's mouth that she instantly stopped talking. Never once had she associated that term with her sister.

After meeting Bu-wi, she'd changed her mind about her sister. She was pretty certain she hadn't committed suicide. The police said it was difficult to tell, but Ki-jeong knew that if she had only known her sister a tiny bit better from the start, then she might have been able to determine the true cause of her death. Because she could do nothing, Ki-jeong had ended it there. But at least now she knew that her sister hadn't simply clung to her past failures.

"Could I see you again sometime?" Ki-jeong asked, as she stood to leave.

Se-oh quietly answered, "Yes."

Se-oh wondered if that question was Ki-jeong's way of saying goodbye or of apologizing for bursting in on her. Death made those left behind suffer; did struggling to understand it help a little? Not because you'd suffered enough and were lonely, but because you'd come to accept the fact that nothing would ever lessen the pain.

Right before stepping out of the room, Ki-jeong asked, "Did Bu-wi like Ha-jeong back?" It looked like the question had just occurred to her.

Se-oh answered without hesitation, "Yes, he did."

Ki-jeong nodded and closed the door behind her. Se-oh did not follow. She didn't watch Ki-jeong walk down the narrow hallway, past the grilled tripe restaurant that was still for lease, past the karaoke bar with its flashing neon sign, and out to the main street. She didn't listen as Ki-jeong's footsteps grew faint. She didn't stare at the crooked chair that Ki-jeong had sat in.

She hadn't told her the truth about Ha-jeong. Because she knew nothing about her. Saying that Ki-jeong could come see her again was a lie. As was her saying that Bu-wi had liked Ha-jeong back. From what she remembered, Ha-jeong had had a crush on Bu-wi and followed him around everywhere, but Bu-wi had not liked her back.

She didn't tell Ki-jeong that they were in the same position. She didn't tell her she often imagined her father's final moments, made conjectures, reconstructed events. She didn't admit that she had ignored the state of things right up until her father's death. She didn't say that, like Ki-jeong, the moment the accident happened, she too assumed the cause of death was suicide. Because, unlike Ki-jeong, she had never attempted to dig deeper into her father's death. All that mattered to Se-oh was the person responsible for it.

Se-oh wondered if maybe Ki-jeong should have waited a bit longer to meet her and Bu-wi. As long as her search for them kept her moving, she could have postponed having to say goodbye to her sister. But Ki-jeong had missed her chance. Now she had to accept her sister's death as an irrefutable fact. The tension would have continued unabated right up until she found Se-oh and Bu-wi. The strange cohabitation with a dead sibling. That was all over now.

Soon that would be Se-oh's life. Once her work was complete, the will to live that had been held in place only by imagining the plan and its execution would flee from her completely.

27

Su-ho was in the grips of an unusual fatigue that would not release him anytime soon. Ki-in Ku's daughter had died. There were various reasons for this. And why wouldn't there be? If the cause of death was disease, then there might be hereditary, physiological factors, and if it was an accident, then there would be any number of coincidences all tangled together.

But Su-ho knew the real reason. It was money. Money had turned Ki-in's daughter's bright future dark and gloomy. He could name ten different examples of this, including himself. He had tried so hard to defy the stereotype of undereducated men raised by poor single mothers. Now he wondered why he'd bothered. Better to have never dreamed of a life spent wearing a nice suit.

Ki-in Ku had always been poor, and so he must have thought that poverty couldn't possibly come knocking at his door anew. But he was wrong. Once poverty knows your face, it never stops knocking. It makes you feel that the longer you live, the greater your debt will grow.

Not understanding the basic causes that had brought him to this point was Ki-in's biggest problem. Ki-in, who should have been busy mourning his daughter at the funeral home, had come instead all the way to Su-ho's workplace because he wanted to find an acceptable reason for his daughter's sudden death. Something other than money or an incompetent father. What he found was Su-ho.

Ki-in kicked the glass door and called out Su-ho's name along with a string of profanities.

On his way past Su-ho's desk to his own, the team leader clucked his tongue loudly enough for everyone to hear and muttered, "Stupid son of a bitch, what a disgrace. How hard did you push him? What're you, an executioner now? Have you no shame? How many times do we have to go through this? I asked you to collect debts, not kill anyone."

It wasn't clear whether the disgrace was Ki-in or Su-ho. Security arrived. As usual, they moved fast. It felt terribly slow to Su-ho, though. The security guards grabbed Ki-in in his black funeral suit. Ki-in cried so hard that he lost control of his body and bent over at the waist, keening. The guards dragged him out. Su-ho watched until he was gone. He watched Ki-in wail and fall to the floor, watched him get thrown into an elevator, watched him beat on the elevator doors as they tried to close until he lost all strength and collapsed, watched him make a spectacle of himself to everyone passing by in the hallway.

Su-ho stole glances at the team leader. As usual, he was wearing a suit perfectly tailored to fit him in the shoulders. Compared to Su-ho's suit, which grew shabbier by the day, his suit grew sharper by the day. Why was that? And why was Su-ho still unable to buy himself a single decent suit despite working so hard? He wasn't some mafia thug beating people up for pay, or a street hustler fleecing people of their money, or a common thief stealing it outright. All he did was go around and collect money that had been loaned to others, and in return a minuscule portion of the money he worked so hard to retrieve went to his paycheck. He showed up for work early every morning, made his tiring rounds outside the office, stayed after hours to work, and even worked on his days off, and yet he was still only scraping by, all while being cussed out and threatened by debtors. He worked his ass off trying to get people to pay their debts, and yet here he was, being treated like a thief, or worse, seen as a killer? His coworkers and even the team leader, who'd taught him everything he knew, looked at Su-ho like he was a murderer, or if not that extreme, then like he was a disgusting beast, or a hideous monster.

The same thing had happened to him last spring. Su-ho was still fairly new to the job at the time. A gas line exploded at the house of a debtor whose next payment was due. He had taken over the client from the team leader only a week prior. The police said at first that it was suicide; later they walked it back, saying there was a chance the explosion was accidental, but Su-ho was still questioned by the police several times. "Well, that sucks. He blew himself up before you could get your money," was all the team leader had to say about it. He didn't rest a comforting hand on Su-ho's shoulder or offer him a handkerchief or go to the police station for questioning in his place. For a while, he even stopped eating with Su-ho or joking around with him. He acted as if Su-ho had personally detonated the gas line.

Su-ho sprang out of his seat so fast that he made himself dizzy. It felt less like he'd stood of his own accord and more like something had shoved him up out of his chair. He had no idea what to do now that he was standing. His coworkers gave him the side-eye as they went about doing their work or taking calls or chatting with each other, all while properly seated. Su-ho remained standing and took a long, hard look at his life. What had happened that he should end up here? And what had made him jump out of his seat just now?

It wasn't the first time he'd felt this way. When he'd heard about the gas explosion, he was so afraid the person was going to die that he couldn't bring himself to visit him in the hospital. He'd gone to the team leader for advice, but all he was told was, "It's your account now, so kill him, save him, I don't care, just figure it out."

He could quit anytime. He could start over anytime. And so he kept going. If nothing else, he felt okay as long as he was working. Sometimes he even got a weird thrill from bullying people and making them shake in their boots. But Su-ho knew they didn't respond that way because he had any real authority; they were simply afraid of getting beat up. Su-ho's problem was that he knew this but was powerless to change it.

Su-ho approached the team leader, who'd long since lost all interest in the matter. The team leader paused in the middle of talking and laughing at someone on the phone to stare at Su-ho. His face hardened as he hung up. Then he jerked his chin at him to ask what he wanted. Su-ho clasped his hands together tightly to hide how hard he was shaking.

"What do you want?"

Su-ho swallowed hard. He was as unsure why he was standing in front of the team leader as he had been a moment earlier when he'd jumped out of his chair. The moment he'd heard Ki-in Ku start to weep and wail, he had wanted to break free from the monster he had become. All he'd wanted was to make a little money, but the cost was too high.

The team leader's eyes bored into him. Su-ho had to say something. His mouth wouldn't open. He dropped his head. The team leader seized that moment.

"Bring me a report of your collection rate from last month."

"Sir?"

"Now, dumbass!"

The team leader's eyes were nearly bulging out of his head. Su-ho took one look and realized that he'd gone too far and maybe the only way out now was to just keep going. He had no idea what lay ahead of him, but at least he knew what was behind him. If he couldn't pay back the money he'd borrowed to get an apartment, then someone else from this same office would come to kick at his front door. Perhaps the one ringing his doorbell would be the team leader. He hadn't personally experienced that kind of suffering yet, but it was easy enough to imagine.

"Ah, okay, yes, sir."

The team leader's face softened and warmed at Su-ho's obedient response. Just how many faces did the man have anyway? Which was his real face? Su-ho met the team leader's eyes and quickly looked away for fear he would think Su-ho was staring at him. He felt that if he looked the team leader in the eyes for too long he might wet his pants.

The team leader had filled him with fear on multiple occasions, but never as badly as when he smiled warmly at him. In that moment, the team leader was money, was business suits, was the future. Su-ho never once forgot the many things weighing so very heavily on his shoulders.

28

The afternoon was filled with things so mundane that it would take effort to remember them. Se-oh was busy enough to not brood over the task awaiting her that night, and yet not so busy that she couldn't listen in on Wu-sul and Jae-hyung's silly jokes. Nevertheless, a scene kept repeating itself inside her mind. Each time it started over, her face hardened and she grew tense.

On her way out at the end of the day, she said to Wu-sul, "I'm leaving now." To Jae-hyung, she waved and said, "Take care." Just as she had every day that she'd worked there.

"Should I not take care?" Wu-sul said with a laugh.

Other days, he'd tried to get her to talk more by saying, "That's the first thing you've said all day," or added something pointless, like, "Go straight home now." Sometimes, to try to get her to smile, he'd asked where she was headed.

This time, when she picked up the pile of empty boxes to take with her, Wu-sul said, "That old lady is working our Se-oh too hard. She should just call a moving company."

Se-oh didn't tell him she was the one who'd volunteered to help. Nor did she tell him it had to be today.

Another family had moved out of the tenement flats the previous weekend. Now only #101 was left. On top of which, Wu-sul had delivered another order of eel to her yesterday. The lady would have spent the entire day simmering it on the stove. When her son got home, she would heat up a bowl of boiled eel for him, and he would eat his late supper in that moist, hot, reeking air.

Nothing was ever certain, of course. Including Su-ho's schedule. She'd spent months tracking the times he came and went. During the week, he usually didn't come home until close to midnight, and an early night for him was still 10:00 p.m. at best. Supposedly he always ate dinner at home on the nights that his mother boiled eel for him, but there was no guarantee it would really happen.

She might even bump into Su-ho. She might greet him as he stepped through the door ahead of schedule, and get flustered and leave #101 without doing anything. Or panic and rush to put her plan into action. The plan in which blue sparks would flare and blossom and everything would vanish in a second. Not even Se-oh would make it out safely.

That thought didn't slow her down, though. She was already as good as dead. She'd died when #157 went up in flames. Since then she'd been a living fossil. Her body had been buried in time. Even if she were to survive this day and be given a new future, that future Se-oh would be no different.

Se-oh hesitated briefly on her way out of the grocery store. She wanted to linger there a bit longer, in that place where Wu-sul and Jae-hyung chatted, laughed often, frowned sometimes, and worried about the future without a trace of pessimism. When she was with them, she found herself wanting to live right. Ordinary tasks and routines made life fun. The two of them taught Se-oh that people are not each other's capital. People existed in diverse forms. It wasn't all good, and it wasn't all bad. There were good times, and there were bad times. Sometimes you could rely on others, and sometimes they disappointed you. Sometimes they filled you with joy, and sometimes they made you angry. That's what normal relationships were.

It all went away the moment the door closed behind her. The world in which she had existed with them was already in the past. Se-oh turned to take one last glance. Wu-sul and Jae-hyung looked very far away.

Tomorrow would find Se-oh gone from this place. She would not go to the park in the morning. She would not watch the old people exercise. She would not trace the arc of shuttlecocks flying through the air. She would not press her back to a wall to hide. She would not wait for the smell of eel and freshwater fish. She would not follow someone with her shoulders hunched.

There would also be no more opportunities to listen to Wu-sul and Jae-hyung's small talk, which was entirely pointless and yet made daily life worth living. She would no longer pretend she wasn't listening only to end up chuckling along. She would not share any more warm, simple meals with them. Conversation would vanish, along with friendly words of comfort and easy smiles. Se-oh was receding from the world of the living. Once she was gone, she would finally ask herself, What on earth had she done with her life?

29

Before redevelopment began, the entire neighborhood had been packed with multi-family flats. The landlords lived on the top floors and filled the lower floors with as many renters as they could. They were called landlords, but they were no better off than their tenants: they lived in fear of tenants moving out before their contracts were up, and then in fear of not being able to find new ones. When the co-op was formed and the plans for redevelopment began to take shape, the tenement dwellers gathered every chance they could, renters and landlords alike, to bemoan their situation, their talk filled with words like variable interest rates, home loans, land valuations, additional contributions, premiums.

Every weekend and every holiday, Su-ho would leave for work in the morning to find his neighbors gathered on the stoop, worrying together about moving and about housing prices. The neighbors who used to respond to his morning greetings by asking after his mother's health or whether he'd looked into moving yet were now all gone. Most had left for other tenement flats on the outskirts of the city.

Su-ho should have done the same right away, but he'd been

delayed when a bank loan fell through. He couldn't afford the deposit on anything else in the area anymore. He had no collateral, and he no longer qualified for credit. His only resort was one of the smaller banks. He had delayed going to one, as he knew that most of the debtors he chased down for payment had done the same thing, but he couldn't put it off any longer. In order not to end up like them, Su-ho's big plan was to pay off the interest without fail and to draw large circles around the dates on the calendar for when he needed to pay down the principal. But he wasn't stupid. He knew the month would come when he would miss a payment, and then, eventually, he would stop being able to pay off any of the interest at all, let alone the principal.

Back when they first moved to this building, he'd thought that they'd hit rock bottom and had nowhere left to go, and so it surprised him to learn that they had no choice but to go somewhere else now. Life was much deeper than he could ever imagine. It was impossible to tell just how far you could sink.

If only his mother were out of the picture, Su-ho thought. Whenever he felt like he was running out of hope, that thought wormed its way into his head. He'd thought it when he saw their last, remaining neighbors move out, too. Every morning when he left for work, he had paused to peek in at the apartments that had emptied out. The belongings his neighbors had left behind were visible through the front window. He could see an old stroller, a preschooler's drawing of the ocean, a Hula-Hoop that had once spun wildly around someone's waist. It looked like people were still living there. Su-ho's apartment looked the same. Like people were still living there.

The debris netting that divided the sidewalk from the construction site began at the subway station exit. In the beginning, it had divided the area into construction zone and residential zone, but by now all of it had become a construction zone, rendering the netting meaningless. The businesses that had taken a big hit while homes were being wiped out in a single stroke stared silently at the barricade as they waited for construction to end and sales to pick back up. With the drop in customers, shops were closing up earlier and earlier, and the neighborhood had grown darker and more deserted. On snowy days, the sidewalks inside the construction zone routinely turned to sheets of ice.

Su-ho headed into the construction zone. It was just past eight. He had gotten off work much earlier than usual because he had skipped one of his regular stops outside of the office. All because of Ki-in Ku. As frightened as his targets were of Su-ho, he was just as scared of them. He assumed that whoever it was who kept calling his cell and home phone to silently threaten him was one of them.

If he hadn't been extra tired and in a hurry to get home, he would not have chosen that path. It was dark and narrow and icy, but also walking that way always spoiled his mood. It made him think bad thoughts. Like how his home was about to get torn down. And about the difficulty of finding a place he could afford with the few coins he had to his name.

His cell phone rang. It was his mother. He didn't answer it. She would be calling to remind him to eat dinner at home or to tell him to come home early. Dinner was probably boiled eel again. He'd warned her that she would have to lay off the eel soup for a while after they moved. The smell inside #101 was terrible. His mother had given up on airing the place out in order to save on their heating bill. Each time she told him she was making another pot, he started to snap, Wouldn't that money be better spent elsewhere? But he always stopped himself. His mother was the only person in the whole world who worried over how tired he was and wanted to feed him something to make it better.

She liked to say, "People are the best thing in the world."

"What's so great about people?" he would ask.

She would look at him in exasperation and say, "What *isn't* great about people? Those who say people are the scariest thing in the world only think that way because they themselves do scary things. But people are good. They can talk. And they can listen. They talk to you. They work for you. They bring you your groceries. They're warm to the touch. And soft and smooth . . ."

Su-ho's favorite thing was money. For that reason, he often became the scariest thing in the world to other people.

Going around collecting on debts even gave him a special opportunity that didn't come often to others. The opportunity to understand people's true natures. The ugly, naked faces that they revealed as they refused to turn over the money. The ease with which they lied.

The bad luck poverty ushered in was close to fate. That is, once you were under its evil spell, everything turned bad. Paying for surgery for a parent on the verge of death. Cosigning for an older brother who was starting a new business. Getting injured on the job when no one else in your family was bringing in any money. No matter how they started, the stories all ended the same way.

Why were life's tragedies so similar? The tragedies Su-ho had witnessed all came down to money. There was nothing more trite and predictable than having no money and no luck. It wasn't the individual backstories themselves, but the way the rest unfolded. Because of money, you'd lose your house, your family, and, in the end, everything.

The penniless liked to weep and bewail their difficult circumstances and apologize for trivial errors in order to appeal for aid. Those people never inspired his sympathy or made him want to help or filled him with compassion. It was simply their own bad luck that had got them there. Su-ho often told them that if they didn't pay off their debts, they would only make things harder for themselves. That they had to pay what they owed in order to live an ordinary life. But it was a lie. They had no shot at improving anything.

Whenever he ruthlessly shook off one of these people clinging to him and begging for help, he felt like he was shoving a drowning person farther underwater. They would die, but Su-ho wasn't the one who'd pushed them into the water in the first place. Dealing with animals had turned Su-ho feral. But he forgot that it was he who had regarded them as animals in the first place.

His legs felt heavy, and he had to piss. He moved over to relieve himself against the netting. He was about to unzip his fly when he heard someone coming toward him. From the sound of their dragging feet, they had to be drunk or maybe just exhausted from work, and yet they shuffled quickly, with urgency. Su-ho stepped aside in embarrassment and waited for the sound to pass. The footsteps stopped. What was this? He glanced behind him. A feeble hand clutched at his arm. If the hand had had any strength to it, if that strength had given him any clue of what was to come, he would have physically subdued the stranger. But the hand that gripped him only held enough strength to ask for directions, to thank a person for steadying them when they were about to stumble, to say sorry for blocking the way. Su-ho was sure that if he turned to look, the person would apologize and walk on with renewed vigor.

The person clutching his arm tipped forward and pressed their face closer to Su-ho's. They smelled. Not of alcohol. It was the smell of eating something spicy and then vomiting it all up. Su-ho turned to brush the person off, but the hand tightened. What was going on? Who was this? No sooner did those questions enter his head than he felt a deep agony. His body shook as if a bucket of ice water had been dumped over him. He bent forward like a broken stalk. He flexed his legs to try to regain his senses. A burning hot something that he could not identify pressed into his stomach again. Then, for a brief moment, the sensation turned to one of cold, as if he were pressing an ice pack to that spot. Had he been stabbed? Was it a knife? Su-ho slowly looked down at himself. A knife quivered there. This was funny. At home they had a kitchen knife that fit into a wooden sheath. Every time he saw it, he thought it was an unnatural way to store a knife. His stomach, which had finally begun to fill out, however, was the perfect spot to stick a knife.

Before the pain spread, his body swayed. Su-ho grabbed the person who'd stabbed him. They did not try to run. They were shaking worse than Su-ho, as if spent from the exertion. They clung to the knife in Su-ho's stomach for support, like it was a kind of pillar. A moment earlier, they'd leaned on Su-ho. Now they leaned on the knife.

It was Ki-in Ku. The spice that Su-ho smelled was the scent of funeral incense. Ki-in was still wearing the black funeral suit that he'd worn when he showed up at Su-ho's office. The mourning suit that he'd worn as he was dragged down the company's hallways. He wore nothing else over it, despite the cold, making him look stupid and poor. It didn't matter how deep your sorrow, how intense your rage. Nothing could stop the cold.

Someone was crying. Su-ho thought at first that it was him, but it turned out to be Ki-in. He sobbed like a little girl. He wept like he'd stabbed himself rather than another human being. Su-ho wanted to tell him to fuck off, but a wave of pain prevented him. Ki-in continued to weep as he reached down to yank the knife out of Su-ho's stomach.

Su-ho's body flared with heat. The pain was overwhelming. His body was a piece of wood that had caught fire. He burst into flame. The heat started in his skin but soon spread to his blood vessels, the blood itself, and each of his organs in turn, or possibly with no sense of order at all. It grew so intense that he lost all track of where the fire had started. Su-ho grabbed onto Ki-in. The other man's body was the only thing he could lean on. But when he felt how hard Ki-in was shaking, he released his grip. Ki-in staggered backward.

Su-ho fell to the ground. A ball of fire was blazing away in his stomach. If he hadn't collapsed, he would have lain down on the cold ground anyway to try to smother the flames. He spat out the saliva that had pooled in his mouth. It dripped down his chin. Slowly, he writhed against the cold ground. The fire did not go out. His stomach still burned. But it was not fire. It was hotter than fire. And yet, strangely enough, his body was growing cold. If he continued to lie there on the bare ground he might end up wetting himself. If you piss yourself, you're done. He could hear the team leader's warning. He tightened his groin but couldn't hold it for long. A hot stream of urine spilled down his thigh.

After starting his job, all Su-ho could think about was money. He even dreamed about it. But they were never dreams of finding money in the street or of someone else playing his regular lottery numbers and hitting the jackpot. A person whose face he could not remember shook a stack of cash in his face. Sometimes Su-ho snatched the money. Sometimes the moment he reached for it, it vanished like smoke. Either way, he never felt all that disappointed. Even in his dreams, Su-ho knew the money wasn't his.

Who was the person who shook a stack of cash at him in his dreams? It seemed like the work of the same person who'd wrapped him in flames and made him piss himself. He would just as soon not remember, and yet countless faces flashed through his mind. Any one of them would have loved to stab Su-ho in the gut. If not Ki-in Ku today, then someone else tomorrow.

The pain made him curl his body up like a larva. His teeth chattered, and his limbs were going numb. All because of money. His mother had been wrong. People were the best thing in the world? If she knew what was happening to him, she would take back those words. If the pain would just let up for a moment, if he could only manage it, he would call and tell her. He would say that people do nothing but lie and make excuses and laugh at you and whine and threaten to kill you and, given the chance, actually kill you.

He didn't know that he was crawling on the ground and crying until he realized he couldn't get up. Blood flowed from his stomach and he'd wet his pants, but that wasn't why. It wasn't because he was afraid of dying. It was because of his great and powerless rage.

30

As the door swung open, a cold darkness rushed out. The apartment looked withered somehow, like a plant long dead and dried up. The only thing still alive in there was the smell.

Se-oh set down the empty cardboard boxes she'd brought with her. The glow of the television illuminated the packed boxes sitting here and there.

"Cold in here, isn't it?"

The old lady had been friendlier to Se-oh lately, perhaps because she'd realized she wasn't going to see her anymore. She had stopped giving Se-oh a hard time whenever Se-oh delivered groceries and had started wrapping up dishes of homemade food for her to take home. No doubt hungry for company after being alone all day, she acted excited to see Se-oh and would find any excuse to make her stay a little longer.

"Did you pack all that by yourself?" Se-oh asked.

"My son did. He must have been so tired after work yesterday, but he did it anyway."

"Have you eaten dinner?"

"I'll eat with my son when he gets home. I've been boiling soup all day for him."

Se-oh boxed up the odds and ends that the old lady handed to her, while the old lady plied her with questions. It was as if they were meeting for the first time. Where did Se-oh live. How old was she. Se-oh answered only as much as she needed to but otherwise did not speak. The old lady didn't chide her for it.

Se-oh sealed the box shut with yellow shipping tape and set it to one side, then picked up an empty box and a pair of scissors and went into the kitchen. The darkness made the gas line look black and hard. Se-oh squeezed it to try to work up her courage. Just the feel of it in her hand made her heart pound. She was certain the old lady would come racing in to scream at her. As if she were capable of racing. Alarmed at the thought just the same, Se-oh stole a peek into the living room. The old lady was sitting on her cushion and watching TV.

She had better get started. The stacks of boxes would keep the old lady from noticing. What Se-oh had spent so long imagining would finally be made real. She pulled on the gas line. Nothing happened. She pulled harder. It showed no sign of budging. At this rate, the scissors would be faster. She knew how easy it was for something you'd wished for to suddenly go sideways. Her heart pounded painfully in her chest.

She gave it another yank. In the dark, it looked like a protruding vein. It was not going to come loose. It may have been old, but it was sturdy. It must have been stuck to that same spot on the wall since the apartment was first built; it was standing its ground as firmly as a support beam. That didn't stop Se-oh, though. She felt a strong sense of duty toward this task. It was time for her to make a decision. Whether to stall while trying to yank out the hose or to cut it with the scissors and leave evidence. Both choices meant risking her life.

She picked up the scissors and stole another glance at the old lady. The woman was leaning to one side, asleep. She looked suddenly ancient. As if every last trace of her youth had expired right along with the deteriorating home that she'd lived in for so long. The television cast its shifting colors over the old woman's hunched shoulders.

Se-oh pictured herself severing the line and opening the valve. A blue spark ignited. A person's living body bled, and everyday objects melted like tears in the flames. The ceiling collapsed, and the furniture burned. A deep hush descended like fog before fear had a chance to set in.

The apartment looked like it had all happened already. It was bleak and gloomy, as if no one lived there. It looked like #157. The same #157 where old timbers had gone up in flames. Where daylight had brought long beams of sunlight muddied with dust and ash. Where the memory of disaster lingered and darkness had crept into every crevice.

Nothing was left of #157 now. With the house auctioned and the new owner chosen, it had become a vacant lot, empty and deserted. Spring would come, but there would be no leaves to stir in the breeze. The trees in the yard had been yanked out by their roots. There were no more red bricks or blue roof tiles, no long-used furniture or broken objects. The earth had been tamped down, hard and serene. Dark shadows did not appear in the sunlight, and black dust did not carry on the wind like the sound of someone's weeping.

"What're you doing in there?"

The old lady still sounded sleepy. Se-oh heard her move toward the kitchen. She set down the scissors and went to join her. The old lady had the phone to her ear and was calling someone. The light from the television mixed with the neon glow of the telephone buttons. "He's not picking up," the old lady muttered. She hung up the phone and turned her eyes back to the TV.

Se-oh sat next to the woman and looked at the veranda window. Dew had collected inside the thick plastic wrap that had been taped over the glass to keep out the cold; the condensation made the outside look murky and gray, like a heavy fog had settled. The longer she stared at the haze, the more she felt like she'd lived this night before. A night spent watching the fog slowly roll in as a smell rose to fill her sinuses. There had never been such a night. And yet she felt sure that she'd been here once before, long ago. She'd waited so long for this moment that it felt like it had already happened.

She committed to memory the dark night, the fog trapped between the inside and outside air, the blurred sounds coming from afar, the bright glow of the television in the darkened house, the foul fishy stench. If she had to choose one single point in her life, it would be this place and this time. No matter how far she went or how much time passed, this was the night to which she would always return. To this fog, this smell, this dark anxiety. To the cold, hard scissors or to the hammer.

The old lady's head nodded as she began to doze off again. She breathed quietly in her sleep. Se-oh covered her shoulders with a blanket lying nearby. Surprised at the kindness of her own gesture, she stared down at her hands. Hands that had taken their time to try to pull out the old gas hose. Hands that had squeezed the valve. Hands that had reached for the scissors. Hands that had packed the old lady and Su-ho's belongings into a cardboard box. Hands that had placed a blanket over the old lady.

What time was it? All she knew was that there wasn't much time left. Now it was time for the darkness to give itself a good shake and increase the concentration of night. Se-oh put on the coat that she'd stashed to one side of the living room and quietly left.

From outside, if she looked carefully, she could see a faint light seeping out of #101. The glow of the TV was blunted by the dew. As it mixed with the trapped moisture, the light grew soft.

Se-oh turned her back on the light and slowly walked away. Toward the place that the darkness made look like an empty void.

ᴇᴘɪʟᴏɢᴜᴇ

Her mother was staring vacantly at the veranda window. Ever since she'd stopped dyeing her hair, claiming that the dye was bad for her eyes, her hair had gone completely white, making her look older and more feeble. Ki-jeong glanced over at her on her way into the kitchen to cook. Their dinners together, with just the two of them, were quiet.

She sometimes thought about the noisy dinners they'd shared when her younger sister was around. There were times when she felt that her failure to properly enjoy those evenings had left her with these too-quiet evenings instead. But it was nothing more than a belated thought. Such regrets were common when someone was gone; they weren't for her sister's sake, but for Ki-jeong alone.

"How was work?" her mom asked.

Ki-jeong automatically nodded yes before realizing that her mother had not asked, "Is work going okay?" She normally asked simply to confirm that Ki-jeong was doing well, but today was different.

"Every day's the same," Ki-jeong said with a smile.

Her mom smiled back. It had been a long time since they did that. Shared a smile.

Ki-jeong had followed her suspension with a leave of absence; having returned to work after a year off, it was, in a word, okay. Every now and then she bumped into the principal in the hallway and would mumble hello. When he was in a good mood, he would respond by commenting on the weather, his hands clasped behind his back. Ki-jeong would follow suit by glancing out the window at the sky and remarking on how clear it was or how it looked like rain. She made no special effort to try to improve his mood or to get an apology for the unfair treatment she'd suffered. The extent of their camaraderie—greeting each other and inquiring after each other's welfare purely out of etiquette—wasn't the worst way of knowing people.

Once she realized that her judgment was not always going to be exact and correct, and that it didn't have to be, she stopped feeling obligated to perform the role of a teacher. She was still afraid of giving her students the wrong impression, but she found the courage to admit when she was not sure or did not know the answer to one of their questions.

Maybe it was the way her mother had phrased the question this time, but Ki-jeong found herself wanting to come clean. After clearing the table, her mother said she was going to lie down for a moment. Ki-jeong followed her into the room. Her mother looked at her quizzically.

She'd gone over it in her mind so many times. How she would begin. When she should tell her. How much she should tell. Contrary to how she'd imagined it, she began with what had happened with her job. After she was done, her mother asked what had become of Do-jun, the boy who'd gotten her in trouble. He was in his graduating year now. She ran into him sometimes in the hallway. His face would turn stony and he would pretend not to see her. She knew, the moment she turned her back on him, he would make fun of her or pretend to take off one of his slippers and hit someone with it, but she never let on that she knew. Nothing had changed. Ki-jeong and the boy both continued to believe their own truths. Nevertheless, it drove home to her the passage of time. It was enough to have realized that they believed different things. Her mother gently stroked Ki-jeong's hand.

Then she brought up her sister. She'd put it off for so long, but once she began talking, it was easy to get the words out, just as it always was when something was finally behind you. She told her mother about holding her sister's funeral alone, about taking legal steps to void her debt, and about all that she'd learned from her sister's friends.

Her mother listened quietly the entire time. She didn't interrupt to ask for more details. She didn't demand to know what something meant or how something had happened. She simply listened. Which was fortunate. If Ki-jeong had had to retell any part of it, she might have lied and said it was all a bad joke, just to get out of it.

All her mother needed now was time. Time to swallow her sadness and guilt and pity. Ki-jeong rose to give her mother some space to herself.

"It must've been so cold," her mother said quietly.

Her tone was gentle, but it was hard to tell what she meant. Ki-jeong looked down at her. Her mother's chin dropped to her chest. Her head hung so low that her neck looked broken. Her shoulders rounded. She brought both hands up to cover her face. Every gesture happened very slowly, as if she were gathering her strength. Quietly, she wept. Ki-jeong stared at her crying mother. Should she put her arm around her, or clasp her shaking hands? She wondered, but did nothing.

Looking at her this way, her mother looked small and so thin that her collarbone stood out in sharp relief. Her once-taut skin had lost its firmness—had probably lost it a long time ago—and faint age spots had spread across her cheeks. Her short hair was stylish but also emphasized her angular face, making her appear peevish and tired.

Ki-jeong sometimes had trouble seeing the connection between herself and her mom, but seeing her up close now, it didn't take any effort. It wasn't because of their facial features that instantly gave them away as mother and daughter. Ki-jeong and her mother sometimes lashed out at each other, clawed at each other, and scared each other. But they were always together. They ate together, folded the laundry as they watched television side by side, went to the bathhouse where they took turns scrubbing each other's backs, after which they shared a small carton of milk and shook out their wet hair before heading home. Other than when teacher training took her away from home, Ki-jeong was always by her mother's side. Maybe that was why her sister was gone while Ki-jeong remained.

Another fit of shivers came over her mother. Though she knew it was not because she was cold, Ki-jeong grabbed a light quilt and covered her with it. Her mother let her. Finally, she realized what her mother had meant when she said, "It must've been so cold." Her sister had slipped into the river in the dead of winter. It would have been freezing, and terrifying.

So much of her mother's life had changed because of her sister. The thought hadn't really occurred to her before. Her mother was only thirty-five when she'd found out about Ki-jeong's half-sister's existence. That was younger than Ki-jeong was now. Learning that her husband had had a baby with another woman would have filled her with suspicion and resentment. She would have become depressed and helpless, and her regrets and her skepticism toward life would have grown. She'd probably felt like her life had been stolen right out from under her. Sometimes she had been unable to overcome her anger at the situation and lashed out at Ki-jeong, beating her. She'd had no one to rely on but her daughter. And so she'd grown vicious, paranoid that her own child was conspiring with someone to make a fool of her.

Her mother and father had stayed together, but as far as Ki-jeong could tell, they lived as little more than acquaintances. They ate at the same table for the most part. Sometimes her mother even hand-washed his underwear for him. Whenever there was a family gathering, they got into the car together, sat next to each other, ate together, and talked and laughed with relatives. When her father died, her mother poured her all into giving him a proper funeral. Ki-jeong had figured it was simply what you did for someone you'd lived in the same house with for so long.

Watching her cry now, Ki-jeong realized she'd had it all wrong. Her mother wept. It was the first time she'd seen her mother weep like that. Ki-jeong held her mother's trembling hand. Her mother did not pull away. It didn't seem like she wanted to hold hands so much as she was too weak to resist.

As Ki-jeong watched her continue to weep, she thought about how her mother used to give her younger sister her daily baths. The look on her mother's face had always been flat and harsh, less like she was bathing a young child than scrubbing a mud-caked, oversized radish. Her mother had regarded herself as the child's babysitter. Though she didn't love the girl, she had probably wanted to raise her just to prove that she could. With the same look on her face as when she did the laundry or the dishes, she'd shampooed the girl's hair and scrubbed off the dirt and dead skin and rinsed her face with water, the girl's eyes squeezed tight to keep the soap out. Without any of the wonder of gazing upon a child's growing body or marveling at how they could chew food with such tiny teeth. No different from scrubbing a stain out of some clothes or a grease spot off of a dish.

And yet, her mother had rinsed off kimchi to feed to Ki-jeong's little sister, who couldn't eat spicy food. She'd taught her numbers and letters with a reluctant look on her face and a forceful tone to her voice. As the girl grew older, she taught her the English alphabet and the times tables. She scolded her when she chewed her nails, helped her to trim her ingrown toenails, and cleaned her ears of wax. When the seasons changed or the child grew, she bought her new clothes. On the first day of elementary school, she went with her to the entrance ceremony. She attended parent-teacher conferences. She signed her report cards, and under the question, "What do you hope your child grows up to be?" on the girl's student records, she wrote in "teacher." When the girl got her first period, she did not congratulate her or start treating her like an adult, but she kept the bathroom stocked with menstrual pads.

During that time, Ki-jeong never once saw her mother laugh or stroke the girl's head or tuck her in at night or speak warmly to her. Her mother did everything in silence, her expression flat. Ki-jeong was grown by then and didn't need that kind of care. Though she loved her and depended on her, Ki-jeong gradually grew apart from her mother. But her sister was young enough to have to depend on their unloving mother.

As the child grew, she began to act free-willed and independent. In truth, their mother and Ki-jeong gave her no choice. She was always there; Ki-jeong and their mother simply refused to meet her halfway, unwilling as they were to grow close. They looked askance at her secret, at the enigma of the girl who would never really be the same as them.

Ever since she'd joined them, their lives had all branched out, away from each other's. It wasn't strange at the time, and it still wasn't. They'd simply realized—her mother through her sister, her sister through her loveless family, and Ki-jeong through her mother—that life had a way of unfolding beyond anyone's control.

Ki-jeong squeezed her mother's limp hand. Her mother was still weeping. She put her arm around her shoulders; this time, as well, her mother let Ki-jeong pull her close. Her mother felt weightless. Only after she became aware that the sense of weightlessness wasn't because her mother was so thin and light but rather because Ki-jeong was leaning on her mother, and that her mother was stroking her arm as if she were a small child, did she finally figure it out.

Ki-jeong knew now what the very first thing was that she should have done for her sister. It was not feeling guilty, or inspecting her phone records, or even tracking down Se-oh.

What she should have done was feel sad that her little sister was gone and would never come back. It should have tugged at her to know that her sister spent her final moments alone. She should have missed her. Just as their mother was doing now. Not because she felt sorry for her, or guilty. Simply because she missed her. That was the first step to mourning.